Trailridge

A Guy Hogan Mystery

Kevin Wolf

Dedication

To Rocky Mountain National Park. Always a place of surprise and magic.

Prologue

July 15, 1982

At 5:30 on a clear morning, a wall of water ten feet high tumbled down Fall River in Rocky Mountain National Park. Trees snapped and boulders toppled like children's toys. The Lawn Lake flood traveled over twelve miles in three hours and devastated the resort town of Estes Park. It is estimated to have caused $31 million in public and private damages, clean-up, and economic loss. Officially, three lives were lost.

There is no mention in any report of a man's body found in Fall River two days before the flood. Nor is there any record of a still-unidentified body that was discovered the day after the deluge.

*I came to the river when anger and loneliness blended.
I came often.*

Chapter One

Rocky Mountain National Park
July 13, 1982

Other fishermen thought this stretch of water was too close to the road. More and bigger fish could be found in the streams and lakes farther into the Park. But the one fish I couldn't catch waited in the pool just ahead.

Where the white riffles swept over the gravelly bottom, the surface of the stream turned slick and smooth. In a pool shaded by the cutbank, each ivory-colored speckle along my trout's sides shimmered.

I slipped to my knees behind a fringe of weeds. Careful to keep my shadow off the water, I swung a four-weight fly rod back over my shoulder, picked the right ripple to place the caddis fly, and arched the rod forward.

A car door slammed.

Across the stream, not twenty yards from where I hid, a woman quick-stepped down the rocky bank from the roadway. Blonde hair fanned over her tan shoulders and a tissue fluttered from one of her outstretched hands.

I glanced away to check my cast. The fly settled on the water, caught the current, and glided into my fish's pool.

The woman stopped in the shade of the trees, just across the stream. Her back was to me. She peered around both sides of a clump of aspens that shielded her from the road, hooked her thumbs into the waistband of her jeans, and wriggled them down.

I didn't know if I should speak. At the least, I should move or rustle the willow branches to warn her that I was there, but the tip of my fly rod quivered. The line drew taut. The trout I'd tried so many times to hook splashed to the surface.

A noise, more surprise than a scream, came from the woman.

I raised one hand to the side of my face, to shield my eyes and let the woman know I wasn't looking. At that second, the rod bent, and the line hissed from the reel. My trout sliced upstream through the swift water. I pulled up on the rod to fight the fish.

"No—o—o." Her sound became a word.

A silver flash cut the water at the end of my line. The trout dove for the dark water at the next curve of the stream. Just as suddenly, the line went slack.

I turned to the woman and shrugged. One of her hands gathered her pants together at her narrow waist. The other pointed up the stream. Strands of hair whipped by the wind caught in her open mouth. Her eyes opened wide.

"I—I—I was fishing. You didn't see me. I didn't mean to . . ."

"No—o—o," she wailed and pointed at a spot upstream from where the trout had freed itself.

I climbed to my feet. Where a deep stretch of water curved, a squat willow spread its branches out over the stream. A pair of pale-colored aspen logs bobbed side-by-side in the current.

Something seemed unnatural. Not right. I stepped forward. One log shifted. The end of the log, pale and white, broke the surface. The fly rod dropped from my hands. The logs were legs. *A person's legs. Someone had fallen into the stream.*

"Get help!" I called and splashed into the moving water.

The woman dashed to the roadway. She waved her arms at a passing car.

The body floated face down. The head and face had caught in the bush's branches. I wrapped my arms around its waist and heaved with all my strength. The dead weight forced me to my knees. Water filled my hip boots. I lunged forward, pushing the body up onto the bank. I scrambled up beside it and rolled it over, ready to force air into the lifeless lungs.

Tentacles of wet hair clung to the man's forehead. Pale purplish lips refused to move. Eyes that had been blue were now glazed with a thick, sticky film.

A chill, colder than the icy water, coursed down my spine. I looked up. The woman from the car had pressed both hands to her mouth. She stared at me for some hope.

All I could do was shake my head.

—

I balanced my fly rod across a trash barrel at the gravel pullout next to the road. *If I had only been more observant—not so focused on the fish—I would have seen the body sooner.* Maybe things would be different. Instead of being stuffed in a black vinyl bag, the man in the stream might be on his way to the hospital.

An ambulance, two Park Service patrol cars, and one from the sheriff's office lined the roadside behind the blonde's red sports car. I found a seat on a bathtub-sized rock. She leaned against her car and crossed her arms. Sunglasses hid her eyes, but her lips trembled. She turned away from the activity beside the stream.

A baby-faced Ranger, in a flat-brimmed Smokey-the-Bear hat, left the others with the body and climbed up to where the woman and I waited. He pulled a spiral notebook from his shirt pocket and nodded at me. "Mister Hogan, I need to get some information for the report, and then you can leave. I'll talk to her first. Be right back for you."

He tucked his Ray-Bans where the notebook had been and straightened his hat. "Miss?"

She turned to face him, caught a thick shock of white-blonde hair in both hands, and raised them behind her head to gather her hair into a ponytail. She was nearly a head taller than the kid-Ranger. Razor-sharp creases had been ironed into her designer jeans, and she wore high heels, more suited for New York sidewalks than the trails in a National Park. Her tank top was silky, ivory-colored, and peaked at her nipples. She was both attractive and confident—almost business-like—despite the circumstances. But I couldn't be sure if the attitude was a weapon or a shield.

The young Ranger shifted from one foot to the other. "Can I see your driver's license?"

The woman turned and stuck her head and arms into the open window of her car. She twisted out of the car, holding her handbag. One hand tilted her dark glasses forward, and she peered over the top of the tortoiseshell frames at the Ranger as if she knew he'd been eyeing her backside.

His best effort at a smile formed on his face. He took the driver's license she thrust at him. "Miss Stanford?" He scrawled on his pad. "Willow Stanford? California license?" Wanting her to answer.

She didn't.

I expected her to tap the ground with the toe of one foot, but she continued to stare over the top of her shades.

"I already talked to the other cop," she said.

"I'm a National Park Ranger, ma'am."

"I told the other *ranger* all this." Lines wrinkled at the corners of her mouth. "I bought a large coffee when I filled the car in Grand Lake this morning. I'm meeting someone in Estes later on. Nature called, and I stopped. I was down there in the bushes when I saw the, uh . . . *body*. He saw it too." She pointed at me. "I ran up here and flagged down a car and told them to call the police." She pushed her sunglasses in place so Ranger-boy couldn't see her eyes. "And I don't make it a habit of peeing beside the road if you're going to try to be cute and ask me that like that other ranger."

"Th—thank you, Miss." He fumbled with her license. She snatched it away, turned to her car, and strummed her fingers on its roof.

I stepped up and handed him my ID and added, "I told Batterton all this. Left my truck about a mile and a half down the hill." I nodded toward Estes Park. "Started fishin' upstream. Like she said"—I tipped my head to the blonde leaning on her car—"I was just down below when we spotted the body. Any idea who he is?"

He handed back my license and shook his head. "They found an Iowa driver's license and credit card in his wallet. Last name was Tait. Mean anything to you?"

"No."

"We haven't found any fishing gear." The kid shrugged. "Tourist out for a hike, I guess. Got too close, slipped, and fell in."

"Somebody misses him." I knew I should feel something, and I cursed myself when I didn't. I'd built walls around my loneliness so tall that few things could climb and long ago I had used up all my tears.

The crew from the ambulance started up from the river with the black vinyl bag strapped to a metal stretcher. The ranger left us and helped haul the sad burden up onto the road.

My eyes closed. The black vinyl became a white sheet, the stretcher, a hospital bed. And this scene beside the river, the sterile room in a hospice. In that second, my numbness opened a rift in the wall, and I knew how that somebody would feel.

Willow Stanford touched my shoulder. "Need a lift to your car?"

—

Most days I preferred silence over small talk, but something inside wanted out. Maybe it was because the body in the stream reminded me of my loss. Perhaps it was because Willow hadn't spoken since she invited me into her car.

"Dashboard looks like something out of an airplane," I said and shifted the sections of my fly rod that rested between my knees.

New plastic and fresh vinyl smells filled the Corvette. Willow swung her car into the line of station wagons and campers headed to Estes Park before the afternoon rainstorms. The tachometer gauge protested the low speeds of the line of traffic. The speedometer hovered below thirty and the gas gauge showed a full tank.

"Nice car," I told her.

"Rental. I picked it up in Denver." She tapped red enameled nails on the steering wheel. A diamond bracelet hung around one wrist, but she wore no rings.

"You staying in Estes tonight?" I thought words might chase away the scene beside Fall River.

"Uh-huh."

"Where?" Wanting her to talk.

Tapping fingernails matched the tachometer. "Standish?"

"Stanley. It's where Stephen King got the idea for

his book—*The Shining*—you know that movie with Jack Nicholson."

She nodded, stared out the windshield, and never looked my way.

"Pull in at the turnout." I told her after the next quiet minutes. "I parked my truck there."

She eased the Corvette into the parking area. I followed my fly rod out of the car door.

"Thanks for the ride. I wish we would have met under better—"

She leaned across the console and smiled for the first time. Perfect teeth matched her perfect skin. Her eyes were a mix of green and brown—like the eyes of the coyotes that stalked the forest near my home. Odd, yet stunning.

She reached out to shake my hand. "Listen, I've been a bitch. That dead man has me all crawly. I never even asked your name."

"It's Hogan. Guy Hogan." Her fingers were warm.

"I'm Willow Stanford. And . . ." She let my hand go and tilted her head, only the slightest bit. "Will I have any trouble finding my hotel?"

I hunkered down on my heels so I could watch her face. I wanted to see those coyote eyes again. "Just stay on this road 'til the edge of town. When it forks, stay to the left. Not more than two miles, you'll see it. The Stanley is a big white place. You won't have any trouble."

"Thank you, Mr. Hogan."

"It's what friends do. And call me Guy."

"Are we friends?" Her eyebrows arched and the coyote eyes smiled at me.

"I tend to make friends easily." It was a lie. My only real friend was an old dog. Once my wife and I had many friends. Being alone suited me now.

Willow never quite looked at me. Those eyes seemed to be searching for something just over my shoulder-like a coyote hunting its prey. "I might need a friend someday, Guy Hogan. I don't have many."

The small talk failed me. I shut the car door, and she pulled away.

After a long minute, I placed my fly rod in the back of my pickup and peeled off my vest and boots. Over my shoulder, the red car moved away down the road.

But something didn't sit right. The gas gauge on the Corvette showed a full tank. Willow had told Ranger-boy that she had bought a cup of coffee when she filled up in Grand Lake. Grand Lake was nearly sixty miles from here. With a gas guzzler like that car, some usage should show on the gauge. It hadn't. She had to gas up somewhere closer. The only place had to be one of the stations in Estes Park.

I had lied about having friends. *Had she lied about where she'd filled the car with gas?*

Chapter Two

Tourists crowded the T-shirt and postcard shops along Elkhorn Avenue. Exhaust fumes mixed with the smell of burgers and fries. A wave of vacationers spilled onto the street after the first showing of *On Golden Pond* at the Old Park Theatre.

A part of me cursed the crowd as locals were expected to do. Another part whispered a prayer of thanks that I could share such a beautiful place with them.

I jammed on the brakes and jerked my truck short of a bald man stepping into the street between the line of bumper-to-bumper cars headed the other direction, but going nowhere. The man gave a sheepish smile and mingled into the current of humanity on the sidewalk.

True locals would shake their heads at the dumb tourist. But locals knew better than to be on Elkhorn at this time of day at the peak of tourist season. After a year, I still had things to learn.

The stoplight blinked to red. The intersection churned

like a river filled with spawning salmon as the crowd scampered for the sidewalk. Red turned green and five cars made it through the light before yellow flashed. In two more cycles of the only traffic light on Elkhorn, I could make the left turn that would lead me home.

Above the lighted storefronts, the July sky chose colors as orange as burnished copper to end the day. Clouds settled like inkblots along the ragged mountain peaks all around the town.

The truck and I rolled forward four car lengths at the next red-to-green change and halted for the wave of visitors surging into the intersection. Swimming against the current of sightseers, Willow Stanford stepped from the sidewalk into the street.

She turned her head and those coyote eyes stared at me through the mosquito splatters on my windshield.

At least, I thought she did.

A splash of bare stomach showed between her tight Levi's and the white shirt she had knotted just below her breasts. Willow stopped beneath a glowing sign that promised *Coors*. She nodded to a woman at the door.

The two could have been sisters.

They were the same height. Even at that distance, the two faces were similar. They shared the same high cheekbones. The same chin. Even the way their hair fell onto their shoulders said the two were related. I wondered if they shared the same coyote eyes.

But something was off. If the two were related, they would reach for each other. Women did that. Jenny always hugged our girls. But Willow stayed a step away. The two did not embrace. Neither tried to touch the other. Instead, the woman reached for the door and opened it. Country music spilled out of the Wheel Bar and Willow followed the woman inside.

Chapter Three

Willow slid into a booth at the very back of the crowded barroom. "Hello, mother," she said to the woman across the table.

There was no greeting. Instead, "You've lost weight."

Willow felt her hips strain against the seams of her jeans and remembered how she had lain on the motel bed as she struggled to tug the zipper closed. Nothing pleased her mother; nothing was ever good enough.

Her mother signaled to a baby-faced, mountain man of a waiter and leaned forward just enough so that the very top of her lacy bra showed at the open buttons of her western shirt. She mouthed the word "martini," and never asked if Willow wanted something to drink.

None of it surprised Willow. When other women her age talked of nips and tucks and having the veins in their legs fixed, Willow's mother married a series of men who could afford the procedures. There had been five so far. Five husbands and five plastic surgeries. Breasts, tummy, two facelifts and eyes.

Willow's father wasn't one of the five. Cadence had left him and ten-year-old Willow in a trailer park in the oil country of eastern New Mexico when it became clear a laborer's wages wouldn't pay for the things she wanted.

Her mother adjusted a turquoise squash blossom necklace, smoothed the front of her blouse, and spoke to her daughter, "*Willow,* really? Why choose that name?"

Willow could react. But she had never won a fight with her mother. Her mother had chosen Cadence for her latest name. But that was five years before and the chance to say anything was long past.

Willow tucked a strand of loose hair behind her ear. "I thought it sounded—you know—sophisticated." It was her little girl voice that answered. The voice that cried on those afternoons and evenings when her mother had left her alone in that New Mexico trailer park.

"And Stanford?" Mother propped her elbows on the table and rested her chin on her folded hands.

Willow swallowed hard and tried to push the little girl away. "A friend from high school went to college there." Something flared. "But you wouldn't know anything about my friends."

Willow's mother reached across the table and laid her fingers on top of Willow's hand. Even on the few times her mother's hand grazed hers, the touch was always cool. "We've both sold pieces of ourselves for what we wanted."

The waiter set a fresh martini on the table. "Something for you?" He nodded at Willow. Willow asked for a Coors.

"Are you sure?" Her mother's eyebrow arched.

"I'm better now." Willow studied the tabletop. "And I'll just have one. I promise."

"Then bring two. In the bottle," her mother told the waiter. "And something salty to go with it." She waved for him to leave and smiled for the first time. It was a practiced smile. Willow was sure. After a moment, her mother spoke., "Have you spoken with your father recently? Or his family?"

Willow's father was in jail. Her mother knew that. Cadence was fishing. It wasn't as if her mother enjoyed gossip. It was more that she collected it like she collected her husbands. She added both to her collection of things she could use.

Willow would not be drawn in. She shook her head.

"Then tell me about your trip so far, *Willow Stanford*." Conversations always happened on her mother's terms. Willow clenched her teeth. "I took the Corvette out this morning like you asked me. I was up there in the park,"—her lips trembled—"and it was horrible. We—they found a man's body. He must have fallen in the river or something."

"That sounds awful." The false empathy and fake sweetness that worked so well with men dripped from her mother's voice. "You didn't see the body, did you?"

"Just for a second—" And Willow told her the story. It was all she could do. Willow was long past hoping for understanding. "After the ranger gave me back my driver's license, I watched them carry the body bag up to the ambulance. I thought I was going to throw up. I gave the man who pulled the body out of the water a ride to his truck. Nice man. We talked some."

"Remember his name?"

"Hogan. Guy Hogan, I think. Why?"

"No reason." Her mother finished the last of her martini and glanced toward the back of the barroom. "Can you excuse me for a minute? I need to make a phone call."

The barman set two Coors longnecks on the table with a basket of pretzels.

"When I get back, I need to tell you about your uncle.

He lives in this little town." She smiled the same smile. "Then let's just be Willow and Cadence. We'll drink our beer right from the bottles and catch up. We have so much to talk about."

'No, we don't, Mother."

Her mother stood and her face disappeared into the barroom's shadows and neon haze until all Willows saw was the smile. "Then we'll make up lies to tell each other and pretend we were happy once. And Willow, just one beer."

Chapter Four

I balanced a bag of groceries on my hip, stabbed the key into the lock, and turned the knob.

"Hey, Zac."

A bundle of black, white, and tan fur galloped onto the porch. The beagle hopped onto his hind legs, front paws swatting at my knees. My hand found the dog's head and rubbed an ear. His pink tongue slurped my fingers.

"I told you I'd be back. Have I ever lied to you?"

The hound trotted to the bottom of the stairs, hitched up a leg, and left a trickle of defiance on the corner of the bottom step.

"That's it, Zac. Let the bears and wolves know who all this belongs to."

The little hound yowled. His tail stopped wagging, and the dog moaned.

"No, Zac, Jenny's not there." My heart let out a moan as sad as the dog's. "You still miss her, don't you, boy?"

I flipped on a light just inside the door of the log house.

Zac scampered across the deck and joined me in the doorway. Lightning flashed on the mountaintops. Faraway thunder rumbled down the valley.

I miss her, too, Zac. I miss her, too.

I pushed this morning's dirty dishes next to yesterday's and filled the cleanest, dirty glass with water. Lights on the answering machine flashed. I hit the button, hoping one of the girls was checking on their old man. It was their turn to call. The machine whirled and spat out the first message.

"Hogan, this is Kent. Need your help. I'm overbooked tomorrow afternoon. Need a guide for an afternoon trip. A man and his son. Kid's maybe fifteen. Neither has ever held a fly rod before. Told them you could have them catching fish in an hour. Call me. I'll be up late—" The machine beeped, and the tape spun.

Message two started. No words, just the click of a hang-up, then a dial tone.

I flexed my tired fingers, took a bottle of aspirin from the grocery sack, and washed two down. The phone jangled.

"Hello."

"Mr. Hogan?" It was a woman's voice.

"This is Guy Hogan."

"This is Deputy Anderson with Larimer County Sheriff."

I saw the dead man at the river again. "What can I do for you?"

"I've been assigned to the follow-up investigation into the body that was recovered this afternoon." Muted music swirled in the background. Willie Nelson sang a lonely song. "Would it be possible for you to meet me in the morning? At the location?"

I felt the cold river water wash over me again. "You mean at Fall River?"

"Yes. I'm not clear on a few details from the report. I thought you might straighten it out for me. Would that be alright?"

Sickness churned in my belly. "What time?"

"Six. Before there are too many tourists on the roads. If that works for you?"

"I'll make it work. I just don't know what more I can tell you that I haven't told someone already."

"I need it first hand is all. I'll see you at six." Click, before I could ask if they'd contacted the man's family.

I called Kent to tell him I would guide the trip the next day and fed Zac. Nothing sounded good to eat, so I cleaned the kitchen. When I plunged my hands into the soapy dishwater, warmth seeped into my achy fingers and loneliness streamed off me like sweat.

When the dishes were put away, I went to the bedroom. The big bed looked empty, so I sank into the La-Z-Boy in the front room and pulled a blanket over me. Zac turned three tight circles and settled into his usual place on the floor near my chair.

—

The best time in the mountains is those few minutes after dawn. Rays of sunlight wash away the dark an inch at a time. In each second, changing shadows paint pictures with colors and shades that no artist could dare imitate. With each dawn, night noises hush, and nothing stirs for a precious few seconds.

Most mornings, Zac and I watched dawn wash away the night. This morning, I was by myself at Fall River.

I rested my elbows on the roof of my truck to steady my bulky binoculars. Across the valley, past Fall River, where the aspens met the meadow, a cow elk with her calf stepped into the sun. Flashes of light sparkled from the river and each ripple lifted a song. Some days the river laughed. Today it wept for the man I was too late to save.

A Winnebago lumbered over the asphalt behind me. The coach labored up the road and belched a cloud of dirty smoke that flavored the mountain air with a taste of civilization.

No sign of Deputy Anderson's car, yet. Or Willow's Corvette.

The deputy would have asked for her to come, too. Wouldn't she?

I rested my hip on the truck's fender and brought the field glasses to my eyes.

The mother elk lifted her head from where she grazed. Her ears twitched, and she whirled for her calf.

Like the blend of thunder and lightning sent by the gods, some force wrenched the binoculars away from my face. The air around my head filled with thousands of tiny sparkling stars that stung my hands as if I'd been attacked by a swarm of angry hornets. The sound of an explosion tumbled over the valley. The chaos focused.

Gunshot. Someone was shooting at me.

—

I dove for the ground and wriggled under my pickup, expecting the next gunshot to tear between my ribs and burst my heart.

Sticky warmth trickled down the side of my face. I touched the spot. Hot pain pricked my skin. I pulled a sliver of glass from my cheek and touched the place again.

Blood. My blood.

I twisted my head and shoulders behind a front tire.

Why? No, think. Not why. Where? Where is the shooter?

I peered around the tire.

Could be anywhere. No. Not in the meadow across the river. Elk saw something. Think. Behind me. On the hill. Shot came from high on the hill behind me.

I made myself breathe.

The side of my face pressed into the dirt. The air I forced

from my lungs skittered grains of dust across the ground.

Think. Up high. Behind me. Aiming at my back. Why? Who?

I sucked the next breath.

Don't think why or who until you know where.

I raised onto my elbows. Over the curve of the tire, I studied a bit of the mountainside.

Go slow. Each rock. Each tree. Don't look at the next until you're sure.

I shifted so I could see higher on the hillside.

Slow down. Listen.

The river gurgled. The breeze teased the grasses. My heart pounded.

Be sure he's not there. And I waited, studying the hillside.

Grit clung to my eyelids. I checked my watch. Six-fifteen.

Deputy should be here.

Scan the hill again. THE WHOLE HILL.

At the far end of the valley, a car came out of the line of trees and followed the two-lane towards where I lay under my truck.

Sit tight. Don't move.

Gravel bit into my elbows. I twisted so I could see the car.

Park Ranger's car.

Breath came easier.

Don't move. Help's coming.

—

The Park Service car downshifted and slowed. As it jerked to a stop beside my pickup, I crawled out from under the truck and crouched in the space between the ranger's car and my pickup. Through the window, Ranger-boy's face was puzzled. "What happened here?"

"Somebody shot at me."

"You sure?" His head tilted like a puppy.

I turned the bloody side of my face towards him and pointed at the bullet hole in the center of my windshield. Glass shards clung to its edges like some hideous spider web. Shiny splinters covered the hood.

Ranger-boy straightened his Smokey-the-Bear hat. "Maybe a rock flew up and hit your windshield?"

"Someone shot at me."

Confusion crowded his face. "Firearms aren't allowed in a National Park, sir."

"Son, I'm tellin' you—you're going to find the bullet that made that hole inside my truck." I pointed to the hill above us. "He shot from up there. Use your radio and get us some help."

He eyed the shattered glass and then the blood on my cheek.

His head swiveled to the hillside. His face went fish-belly white. "Holy crap."

Yeah, holy crap.

—

Like yesterday afternoon, two Park Service patrol cars and one from the sheriff's office took their places along the roadside. Ranger-Boy stood in the center of the two lanes of asphalt and motioned for cars full of gawking tourists to keep moving.

National Park Law Enforcement Ranger, Click Batterton, fumbled with a Polaroid and snapped his last pictures of my truck. He tipped his head at the kid directing traffic. "Taylor, there, thought he was gonna protect Bambi and do campfire talks 'bout how wildflowers grow. Drowned man yesterday and gunshots this mornin'. You're gonna have him wondering what he signed up for, Hogan." He set his camera on the hood. "He's punctual.

I'll give him that. If he wouldn't have been on time for his patrol, you might still be under that truck of yours."

Batterton hooked his thumbs in his belt. "For all that just happened, you're awful cool, Hogan." He studied my face. "Been shot at before?"

"Korea. You?"

"Seventh Marines. They sent us winter campin' at Chozin."

"Heard that was tough."

"It was that." Batterton caught my chin and tilted the side of my face up. "You ain't hurt bad, but best to have one of those sweet young things at the hospital take a look."

"It's just a scratch." I pushed Batterton's hand away.

"You're goin' to the hospital, Hogan." It was an order, not a suggestion. "I'll need it for my report." He let go of my face and leaned a hip against his patrol car. "I could understand if this was in the fall. Every once in a while, some goofy hunter sneaks into the park and starts blastin' away at a deer. But not this time of year."

"This wasn't an accident." I nudged my ruined binoculars with the toe of my boot. "The bullet hit my binoculars and ricocheted into the truck. A couple inches the other way and it could've been the back of my head." I dabbed my cheek with a kerchief. "What I don't understand is why he only shot once."

Batterton rubbed the gray stubble on his chin. "We've sent for a tow truck. The deputy is going to haul your pickup to the crime lab in Fort Collins and see if they can find that bullet. I'll give you a ride to the hospital. And Hogan—" he bit down on his lip "—Deputy Anderson?" Batterton looked away before I could speak. "No one named Anderson works for the Larimer County Sheriff's Department 'cept a sixty-three-year-old file clerk everybody calls Miss Susan."

Chapter Five

Cadence Tait studied her face in the mirror over the hotel dresser. She turned slightly and lifted the hair from her forehead. The tiny creases at the corners of her eyes that her third husband had paid the best plastic surgeon in Tulsa to remove had returned. Perhaps it was the stress of the last few days. But she could pick out each shiny scar from number four's facelift in the hairline above her ears. But most of all, she hated how her top lip seemed stiff and frozen. No matter how much lipstick or which shade she applied, her lip stayed waxy and motionless. Almost corpse-like.

She hated that lip.

Surgeons could shape the skin and tighten the places where muscles had gone slack. Dentists would cap, straighten, and bleach the years from teeth. Hairdressers did wonders at the camouflaging the gray. But that lip betrayed her.

Her daughter had looked so wonderful last night. Fresh.

Natural and young. Cadence would have to schedule a time to talk with her surgeon once all this had settled.

The mirror turned every small discoloration in her skin into giant liver spots. She snatched up a makeup brush from the dresser top. Another brushstroke touched the tiny flaw on her cheek. Tissues wiped away the lipstick until the next shade darker could replace it. A bit more spray corrected the mussed places in her hair.

Only then, she allowed herself to pick up the phone. Cadence pressed zero, looked back at the mirror, and touched the brush to her cheek again.

"Front desk. How may I help you?"

"This is Cadence Tait. Room two seventeen." She checked her ears. She must change to a smaller earring. The weight of the jewelry she wore caused the skin on her earlobes to sag. "I checked in late last night." She pushed concern into his voice. "My husband. I thought he was with friends. He never came in last night. I've called his friends and they say he was never there." She ratcheted up her voice. "His car's not in the parking lot."

"Ma'am, I, uh, I don't know. Should I call the manager?"

"Please." She rolled her eyes that the young woman could be so dense. "And notify the police."

—

"This is Cadence Tate," she said into the phone and pushed yesterday's copy of the *New York Times* to the side of the hotel bed.

"Mrs. Tate, my name is Michael Sanchez. I'm the Chief of Police here in Estes Park."

"You have any news about my husband?"

"He's at the hospital. One of my men is on his way to pick you up—"

"Is he—"

"An officer is on on the way. We'll talk at the hospital."

She checked her makeup in the mirror. "Is my husband all right? I demand an answer."

"I'm sorry to have to tell you this . . ."

Chapter Six

I put my fly rod, waders, and the rest of my gear in the back of Batterton's patrol car. The ranger flicked a switch on his radio as I slid into the front seat.

"Batterton, here." The lines around his eyes wrinkled like the worn places on the leather of an old Bible. "I'm goin' to run Hogan to the hospital in Estes. Anything goin' on in my park I should know about, Sonny?"

The radio clicked and a faraway voice hissed back. "Accident at the Rock Cut. Some dumb tourist thought the gap looked too narrow and was straddling the center line. You know what happens up there, boss."

"Got mixed up with an oncoming car, huh? Anybody hurt?"

"Not this time. They saw each other in time and took to the ditch. Traffic's backed up. They're waiting for a wrecker from Grand Lake to get up there and jerk 'em out." The radio crackled. "How many times has that happened so far this year?"

"I've lost count. And it's only July." Batterton started the engine. "Sonny, if you need me, I'll be at the hospital, like I said." He flicked the radio off and pulled his car out onto the road. One hand, with skin as rough as pine bark, steered while the other tucked a pinch of Skoal into his lip. Batterton looked at me. "Hogan, I can't figure who'd take a shot at you. Maybe some idiot decided to do some target practice."

"Why just one shot, then? Somebody out for fun would crank off a bunch?"

He shifted the tobacco in his mouth. "Maybe it was some kid. Popped a shot off and saw he hit your truck and lit out of here." The old ranger kept his eyes fixed on the road. "We'll find him."

"That doesn't explain the call from Anderson."

"I've been studyin' on that "—Batterton glanced at the road for a long minute and then back at me—"and I don't have an answer yet."

I made up my mind that as soon as I was finished at the hospital, I wanted to get back to the park and see what I could find on the hill. Footprints. Shell casings. The shooter would have left some signs.

Batterton lifted the pop can to his lips again and let the worn-out tobacco drip in the can. "If you're thinkin' of doin' anything more than lettin' me do my job, I'm tellin' you to cut it out right now." He made a clucking noise with his tongue. "If that bullet woulda killed you, the FBI gets the case. Murder in a National Park, you know. If they find a bullet and figure out who shot at ya, it's an assault. That goes to the county sheriff. Right now, all we got is—maybe, unlawful discharge of a firearm and maybe vandalism to your truck. That means it's mine." He adjusted the tobacco in his cheek with the tip of his tongue. "I hope they find the bullet soon. I hate paperwork."

—

"Just six stitches." I turned my face so Batterton could see the repaired cut on my face. "Hardly worth the time." I filled a coffee cup from a pot on a counter in the hospital waiting room. "You promised me a sweet young thing. That nurse was almost as old and dried up as I am." I took a sip. The coffee was barely warm. "You gonna give me a ride home?"

Batterton looked up from his coffee cup. "Plans just changed. While you was gettin' doctored on, I got a call from the Estes Police. A woman reported her husband missing. He matches the description of the man you pulled out of the river yesterday." The ranger dropped his cup into a wastebasket. "They're bringing her up here now to have a look at the body." He peered at the top of his boots. "No matter how many times I've had to do this, it still puts a kink in my guts."

I gulped the half-warm coffee, wanting it to chase the bile back down my throat.

"No tellin' how long this might take." Batterton lifted his face and looked at me through hooded eyes. "Better call somebody for a ride, Hogan. This is just too soon. Not even been a year since you lost your wife."

I curled my bottom lip over my teeth and bit down. "Ten months," I said, more to myself than to Batterton. *And seventeen days.* I looked out the door. "I'll wait outside. Let her know I was the one who found the body. If she wants to ask me anything, I'll be glad to talk to her."

—

An Estes Park Police car rolled to a stop at the hospital's front door. From the corner of a bench near the entrance, I watched the uniformed officer jump out and run around to the passenger side. He opened the door and held out his hand to help a woman from the car. She pushed his hand away, and the day turned lukewarm like my coffee.

The woman I had seen with Willow outside the Wheel Bar was there to claim her husband's body.

Chapter Seven

Cadence Tait let her shoulders slump and never raised her eyes. Instead, she studied the ground in front of her. The Estes Park policeman led her into the hospital. A man in a starched tan uniform and straw cowboy hat stepped up as she entered the lobby.

"Mrs. Tait?" He took off the hat and held out his hand. "We spoke on the phone. I'm Mike Sanchez. Chief of Police."

Cadence nodded.

"I know this isn't easy," Sanchez went on, "but we have no other way." Sanchez waved to a man in the gray shirt and green pants of the National Park Service. "I'd like you to meet Click Batterton. Click's a law enforcement ranger. He was there when they recovered the . . . uh . . . the man's body. Because this happened in the park, he's part of the investigation."

Cadence reached out to take Batterton's hand.

"I'm so sorry," the ranger said.

The words came so clumsily that Cadence was surprised the man didn't stutter. She had spent most of her life around simple men like these. The police chief, she guessed, had been appointed by the town council. No doubt, he'd settled for the job in this small town because he wasn't up to something better. And the ranger was just another government employee, doing his job, and guarding his pension.

"The coroner is waiting for us. This way." Sanchez guided her to a set of doors at the back of the lobby. When Sanchez put his hand on her arm, she wondered if he would have done the same if she were a man, but she resisted the urge to pull away. The ranger opened the doors and stepped back as Sanchez led her down a long hall. The smell of cleaning chemicals and disinfectants hung so thick, it prickled her nostrils and she fought the urge to sneeze.

Their little group stopped at the last door in the hallway. The ranger took a manila envelope from a metal shelf on the door, opened it, and dumped the contents into his cupped hand. "Mrs. Tait—"

"Cadence, please."

"Alright, *Cadence,* do you recognize these?" There was a quick introduction to a man in a lab coat. Sanchez said the man was the coroner's assistant. He opened his fingers. Two rings rested in his calloused palm.

"There my husband's." She muffled a gasp. "His wedding band. The other is his class ring. University of Iowa 1937. He never took them off."

"They were found on the body." The ranger pressed on the door. It swung open, and the four went inside.

Cadence had expected the body to be in another room and them to be behind some window, but it was not at all like television. She cursed the small town.

The police chief stepped to the other side of the table

and the ranger stood near the head of the sheet-draped body.

"Let's get on with it," she said.

"I must warn you. The body was in the water for some time. Whatever you prepared yourself for—well, it's gonna be much worse," the old ranger said. "And I apologize for the smell," he added as if he were testing her. "Bodies decompose quickly once they've been in the water."

Cadence refused to be shaken. She let out a long breath. "I'm ready."

The man in the lab coat lifted the sheet.

She wasn't prepared for the greenish tinge. From being in the water, she suspected. So mottled. So ugly. So much for her latest husband. She found a clean place on the sheet just above his shoulder and stared at the spot. She didn't want to look at him anymore. He'd served his purpose. The seconds passed. When she felt the time was right, she told the men in the stuffy little room, "That's my husband."

Then she made the tears come.

Chapter Eight

I moved into a bit of shade outside of the hospital and watched the dead man's wife through the front doors.

Was I sure it was her I'd seen with Willow?

I stepped closer and strained to see through the glare on the glass. Batterton and Mike Sanchez met her in the center of the waiting room. Batterton shook Willow's friend's hand and gestured to a set of doors at the far side of the lobby. When Sanchez took the woman's arm, I thought she was going to pull away, but she followed Batterton through the door into the hospital.

My empty stomach turned over. I grabbed a handrail near the front door to steady the weakness that found my knees.

Was that the woman I saw on the street?

I replayed the scene again outside of the Wheel Bar. And again. Then once more and five times more.

It was her.

I had no doubts.

But *who do I tell?*

The cop who had driven the woman to the hospital set his coffee cup on the information counter in front of a giggly, blond volunteer who probably wasn't out of high school. She flipped the ends of her hair and he flexed his chest.

I'd wait for Batterton.

—

It was over forty-five minutes before Batterton stepped back into the lobby. He was by himself. Before he could stop at the coffeepot, I tapped on the glass and waved for him. He filled a cup and came outside.

"You still here?" he asked, sipping his coffee.

"I need to tell you something."

He raised his chin. "Remember somethin' you didn't tell me this morning?"

I shook my head. "You need to hear this." I tipped my head toward a picnic table under a pine tree between the hospital's front doors and the parking lot. The ranger followed me over.

Batterton dug into his shirt pocket for his Skoal, filled his lip, and added a gulp of coffee to the mixture. "What is it, Hogan?"

A breeze rustled the pine needles above me and turned the sweat on my back clammy. "That woman who was with me when we found the body—said her name was Willow Stanford. I saw Willow downtown last night with her. They went into the Wheel Bar together."

"Her, who?"

"The dead man's wife."

He cocked his head and stared at me, open-mouthed. "One more time, Hogan. Slow. So, I'm sure I get it."

I drew in a deep breath. "I saw Willow Stanford with the woman you just took back to see the body. They were outside the Wheel Bar last night. They seemed to know each other. They stood there for—justa, you know—a minute. Then went inside."

"You sure?"

"I'm sure."

"How sure?"

I looked him in the eye. "Positive."

Batterton leaned forward and grabbed the picnic tabletop with both hands. His head drooped forward, and his shoulder blades made tents in the back of his uniform shirt. He raised his face and looked at me. "Do you know who that woman is?"

—

Cadence Tait waited while Mike Sanchez opened a side door to the hospital. The two stepped into the sun and Cadence let the day's warmth melt away the coolness and smells of the morgue. The police chief gestured towards his car and as she followed him, she began to check off items on her mental list.

Must call Paxton's assistant and have her notify the mortuary. They would make arrangements to get the body back to Iowa. Sooner would be better. *Next, call Paxton's son.* He was stoic, like his father. She'd have the stepson call his sister. Cadence didn't want to bother with the silly girl's tears.

Sanchez opened the police car door for her. Over the top of the car, she spotted two men at a picnic table near the hospital's entrance.

She touched Sanchez's arm. "What did you say the ranger's name was?" She dabbed at an eye. "I've forgotten already."

"Click Batterton."

"Click? That's an odd name."

"It's a nickname, I'm sure. Never heard anyone call him

by anything but that. I know he was in the Marines. He said he was an artillery spotter. I think it has something to do with that."

"I wouldn't know about such things." She lifted her eyes. "The other man?"

"That's Guy Hogan. He was the one that found your husband's body."

The blood turned icy in Cadence's veins. She felt her body shudder.

"You okay ma'am?"

"Everything is beginning to weigh on me." She'd let out a sigh she was sure the police chief would hear. "Should I thank Mister Hogan?"

"Hogan lost his wife to cancer about a year ago. They were building a home here in Estes. She died just after they moved in. He keeps to himself, ma'am. Like he's waiting for the mountains to heal his hurt. I can introduce you—"

"It's probably best we leave him alone." Even at the distance, Cadence studied Hogan's face. She slid into the police car. "Poor man," she said, just loud enough for the police chief to hear.

—

I watched the police car leave the hospital parking lot and shook my head.

"Hells bells." The words tumbled out of Batterton in some concoction of confusion and desperation.

"Should I know her?" I asked.

"Her husband is some muckety-muck from Iowa. The governor's best friend and all that. They were gonna make him a senator until—"

"I remember now. It came out his wife was a stripper?"

"Had been an *exotic dancer*. And that was three husbands and twenty years before. Cadence is her name. Shit, even sounds like a stripper's name." Batterton lifted on the edge of the picnic table until the tendons in his neck drew the bowstring taut.

Flashes of *People Magazine* covers at grocery store checkout and network newscasts focused in my head. I recalled the businessman with a much younger wife. I tried to match the face of the woman at the door to Wheel Bar and in the hospital with the woman in news stories and magazine covers. *Maybe, just maybe.*

Batterton went on, "They were big news until the British started shooting at Argentina in the Falklands. Cadence— the wife—even said something about that."

I remembered. "That she wished it was a bigger war. So reporters would get the cameras out of her face." That face matched now. "I lost track after it dropped out of the news. Why are they here in Estes?"

"She told us her husband came by himself to do some fishing before he's supposed to be sworn in as the senator. She came to join him yesterday. He's not at the hotel. She reports him missing. And—" He settled onto the table's bench and shook his head. "Are you damn sure?"

I swallowed. "I'm sure."

"This whole thing is startin' to get a stink to it." He pointed at the bench across from him and said, "Sit down and I want to hear it all again. Don't leave nothin' out."

When I finished telling Batterton about the car ride with Willow and what I'd seen downtown, he strummed his fingers on the table and looked up. "Sanchez said that Cadence claims her flight from Iowa landed in Denver about three. She had dinner with friends and didn't get to Estes until close to two in the morning." He looked at me. "Yeah, that's after you saw her with . . ."

"Willow."

"Yeah, Willow." He pinched the skin between his eyes as if to coax his next thought free. "Don't say anything to anyone else. I'll tell the police chief what you told me. I'm sure he'll want to talk to you and hear it for himself." He rubbed his chin. "What're you doin' for the rest of the day?"

"Kent asked me to guide a fishin' trip."

"Go ahead and go fishin'." He looked over his shoulder, spotted the policeman coming out of the hospital, and waved for the cop to join us. Batterton forced out a hoarse whisper. "Hogan, there's probably a good reason for all of this. Hell, maybe it wasn't her you saw with that girl."

"It was her."

"Okay, I believe you. Now sit on this until you hear from me or Sanchez." He nodded. "That cop'll take you home."

"Nah, have him take me to Kent's Flyshop. I'm going fishin'."

Chapter Nine

Mike Sanchez pulled his patrol car into the fire lane at the rear entrance to the Stanley Hotel. "Again, I can't tell you how sorry I am."

It was the twelfth time the man had said the exact same thing. Cadence had counted.

She stepped out of the police car. Clean air, so different from the stodgy, chemical smells of the hospital, brushed over her face. She turned to the policeman. "One of the things my husband enjoyed most was the mountain air. He said it was light and fresh compared to the thick, humid air in Iowa."

Cadence stood there a moment and shook her head, trying to chase away the image of the body on the table. But the wrinkled, green flesh stayed. Before she mashed her eyes shut and nodded to the sheriff, she imagined that the water had washed all but the green from the man's skin and that she could see her bones through some translucent membrane.

The image was a hindrance, nothing more.

"Can I walk in with you?" Sanchez asked.

"That won't be necessary."

Cadence walked to the hotel door. Over her shoulder, the police car left the parking lot. For the first time since she'd left her room nearly five hours before, Cadence Tait allowed the slightest smile to curl the corner of her lips.

Chapter Ten

It should have been the kind of trip that was a pleasure to guide. Not a cloud in the sky anywhere, no one on the stream except us, and a father who was more interested in having his son catch trout than catching any himself. I had chosen a spot on the other side of the park from where I'd found the man and from where someone had shot at me. But each time I studied the next bend in the stream for fish, I saw the man's body again. Too many times, my mind made the chirps of the birds in the aspens on the hillside into the sound of a rifle bolt shutting on a live cartridge.

"Once more, Todd." I stepped away from the teenager and watched with the boy's father. "Just like before."

The kid swung the rod back to ten o'clock, paused, and arched forward to two. Line slid through the guides and the fly settled on the water without a splash. In an instant, water saturated the feathery bundle, and the fly sank, caught the current, and glided down the stream.

"Be ready." I studied the stream's surface. At the place

where the thick fly line met the nylon leader, the line twitched. "Now."

The boy jerked the tip of the fly rod up. The line went taut, and the trout splashed to the top of the water. "Dad," he called out.

His father slipped the net into the stream and lifted the struggling fish. "I think this is the biggest one yet. How many is this? Five?" The man winked at me.

"No, Dad. That's six. I caught six fish today."

"I guess I lost count." A smile as long as the river curled the father's face. He stepped closer to his son and held the rod as his boy took the fish from the hook and gently released the trout back into the stream.

The prickly feelings that ran up and down my back eased, and I wanted the minute to last longer for the dad and son. "I got an idea," I told them. "If you're willing to take a hike, there's a beaver dam about a mile from here. This time of day there just might be a big ole fish cruisin' around down deep where it's cool. He'll be tough to catch. Fish don't get big by bein' stupid. We'll have to sneak up on him."

"Can we, Dad?" The boy's face burst into an even bigger smile.

Todd's father looked at me. "You sure? You already stayed an hour longer than we paid for."

I winked. "I'm havin' as much fun as you guys. Follow me."

We slogged through the swampy grass along the stream and crossed through some waist-high willows until we found a game trail that led to a grove of aspens on the side of the hill. Clumps of red Indian Paintbrush crowded around a matchstick tumble of fallen aspen that the beavers had worked over. Yellow and blue wildflowers dotted the meadow, and swarms of gnats rose around us with each step.

"Ugh, bugs." Todd gagged and swatted at his face.

"That's why we fish with flies," I told him and brushed away a deer fly that tried to perch on my lip. "Just a little bit further."

Magpies cackled somewhere ahead, and I strained to hear the sound of the stream through the willows that choked the creek bank. I motioned for Todd and his father to step in closer. "It should be just ahead," I whispered and moved Todd in front of me. "We'll go in single file. Todd, you lead. When we get to the pond, I'll point where I want you to cast. Relax and lay the line out there just like you've been doin'. You'll only get one chance at a lunker." I hoped I'd planned things right, and I hoped a big fish was waiting. A big, hungry fish.

Another deer fly buzzed my ear. "Ready?"

Todd's father touched my elbow. "Guy?" He pointed up the hill. "See that?" he whispered.

Maybe twenty yards from where we stood, a swatch of green grass and flowers came alive in a swirling cloud of motion. A faint buzzing ratcheted louder and louder as the hungry flies left whatever they had been feeding on.

And the sweet, sickly smell of death turned my stomach.

—

Todd poked at the animal with the tip of his fly rod. "It's gross. What do you think killed it? Mountain lion?"

"Not sure. Could be any one of several things."

I didn't like what I saw. Except for the shiny hide swollen to near bursting, the smell that perfumed the summer day, and eyes pecked away by the magpies, the elk looked healthy. No signs it had been in a struggle. No claw marks or broken legs. But my eyes found a red hole, no bigger than a quarter, that had punctured its ribs just behind its front shoulder.

"Listen, Todd." I glanced at his father to see if he saw

what I did.

The father slapped at a swarm of flies and stepped back.

"Todd," I said again. "I'll stop at the ranger station on my way back to town and tell them what we found here." I tilted my head toward the beaver pond in the willows below. "What say we see if we can catch that fish? It's getting late."

Todd and his dad backed away from the dead elk and swarming bugs. I hung back a moment longer. There was something else. I'd seen it when we found the elk, but didn't want to alarm the father and son.

Besides the bullet hole in its side, someone had sawed off the bull's antlers.

I wondered if the bullet in the elk would match the one in my truck.

Chapter Eleven

The list of things she should not have done was a long one. Visiting her mother's brother might be added to that list. She knew it was a test.

Willow used the map her mother had drawn on the Wheel Bar's napkin to find the turnoff. The tips of the grass in the center of the two-lane road brushed the underside of the Corvette as she edged through a stand of pine trees to where three pickup trucks filled a narrow swath of packed dirt in front of a tired cabin. She parked in a patch of weeds, in the shade of an old shed, and let the car's engine run so she could enjoy the air conditioning for an extra minute.

These mountain people would be like the oilfield workers and ranch hands she'd grown up with in New Mexico, she guessed-predictable and boring. Those working folks never used the front door. When you came to visit, you used the back door that entered the kitchen.

Willow climbed three wooden stairs at the side of the house, pushed open a screen door, and stepped into a shadowy kitchen. Strands of cobwebs brushed across her face. Petrified mouse turds crunched on the linoleum under the soles of her boots. From the light of a single bulb over the cluttered table, she could see where the rodents had left their droppings on the tabletop.

She could see the family resemblance. Her uncle was a tall man. His face was tanned and etched with leathery creases from working outside. She wondered for a moment if her mother's skin would be just as wrinkled if not for the surgeries and potions she spent so much of her husband's money on.

Her uncle leaned on the edge of the counter. He was not so much watching as he was studying her. It was her mother's order, she was sure. But the test was his. Studying to see if she'd cringe like some little girl frightened by a spider.

So, Willow ran her index finger over the kitchen counter, lifted it to examine the dirt, and smiled. The one thing she could be certain of was that her mother had demanded something like this and was waiting for a report.

Her uncle drew a tight circle on the inside of his cheek with the tip of his tongue. "This is, er"—he paused—"Willow, yeah. Willow," he told the three men around the table.

A lanky man crushed a beer can in his fist and Willow felt his eyes sweep over her. The other two were much shorter—take away another two inches or so and they could be dwarfs. Both sipped their beer and, in some strange unspoken communication, it was as if one had told the other to never take his eyes from the rubber-banded rolls of bills on the kitchen table. The other little man studied her tight jeans.

The money was there for her benefit, she guessed. Why else?

Her uncle turned to her. "You're early."

"Mother told me not to be late."

He tilted back his orange and blue baseball cap. "Give me a minute."

Her uncle turned back to the men. "Which one of you killed the big eight-pointer? Those antlers will bring a bunch."

"It was me," the tall man said. "Those two,"—he nodded at the dwarfs—"had a bunch spotted on the top of Deer Mountain. I thought if I took my time, one of those old bulls might try to slip out the back." He rolled his shoulders, and Willow could hear his neck pop. "Just hid out and waited for him to give us the sneak. That bull never knew where I was. Came within ten yards of the devil. Shot 'em in the ear with a twenty-two pistol. Took four steps and dropped over dead." Usher licked his lips and eyes played over Willow.

Her uncle picked up the largest roll of twenties from the table and held it out. "Hayden," he said.

One of the little men snapped the money from her uncle's hand. He twisted away the rubber band and thumbed through the bills. He looked at his counterpart and nodded. "It's all here." Both stood. Rusty-colored blotches smeared the fronts of their dirty T-shirts and stained the legs of their pants. Each took up another beer from the twelve-pack on the table and walked away. Neither said another word as they shut the door behind them.

"Here's your share, Usher." Her uncle tossed the last bundle to the tall man.

Usher plucked the money out of the air and tucked it in the front pocket of his jeans. He looked at Willow and let a smile curl his lips. "Nice car." He tilted his head toward the streaked kitchen window. Stray dust motes danced on his breath.

"On your way, Usher," her uncle said. He brought himself to his full height.

"Maybe you could take me for a ride sometime." Usher

never looked away from Willow.

"You got your money, now get out here," her uncle said.

"Just bein' friendly, that's all."

"Now."

"Okay, okay." He paused in front of Willow. "I ain't jokin' about wantin' a ride."

Unlike the two little men, Usher's T-shirt was clean and the only blood stains were on his hunting knife's leather sheath. He paused again at the door.

"Get out, Usher." The tendons in her uncle's neck tightened.

Usher took a long, last look at Willow and winked as he closed the door behind him.

Her uncle pinched the skin between his eyes. His shoulders sagged like he'd worked hard all day and needed to rest. "Don't pay any attention to that one."

"I'm used to it." It wasn't a lie. She filed Usher's name and face into that place in her head where she kept track of men like him. Men that could be used.

"I bet you are." Her uncle raised his chin towards the red Corvette parked near the shed in his side yard. "You should do something about that car. It sticks out like a sore thumb."

"You sound like my mother."

"Is that a compliment?"

"No." Willow brushed the dirt and droppings from the tabletop with her sleeve and settled onto a kitchen chair. She took the last beer from the twelve-pack on the table. The beer was warm, but she popped the tab and tipped the can to her lips. It wouldn't be the first warm beer she'd drank. "Mother said you would explain everything. I'm here to listen."

He took two water glasses and a bottle of Crown Royal from a cabinet over the sink. He held out the bottle to her.

"Not now," she said as sipped her beer. "I'll have some

later."

He shrugged and sloshed the whiskey into one of the glasses. "How much do you need to know?"

"Everything. Especially about the money."

He took a gulp of the whiskey. He tipped down the bill of the baseball cap and began. "Usher runs the operation on the west side of the park. The brothers hunt this side. They're good at what they do . . ."

Willow raised her hand to stop him. "The money," she said, "tell me about the money."

"Okay, but I don't have much time. I got someone I need to see."

—

Cadence Tait set the room service tray on the floor outside the door. She'd been careful to pick at her food like she supposed a grieving spouse should. What a shame. The trout had been quite tasty.

She filled a wineglass and took a seat at the small desk near the window. Clouds hid the setting sun behind the mountain peaks, and golden sunbeams flooded the valley. Perhaps this was the beauty her husband had raved about so.

She took the phone and dialed.

His secretary picked up on the second ring.

"Audrey, this is Cadence."

"Oh. How are you doing?"

"Fine—considering." Cadence held the phone close to her lips to be sure Audrey heard her sigh. "The people here are very—*understanding*. How are the arrangements coming?"

"Paxton's—I mean, Mr. Tait's son has everything worked out with the mortuary. They'll meet the plane when the bod—Oh, my. I'm sorry." She thought Audrey was going to cry. *Again.*

"That's fine, I understand. Thank you for staying late and handling all this. Now, did our broker happen to leave a message?"

"Yes. I wrote down what he said. I can fax it to the hotel."

"No, Audrey. Just read it to me."

"Are you sure? You must have a lot on your mind now."

I'm sure, you silly woman. "Please." She tapped her enameled fingernails on the desk. "I need to think about something other than Paxton, even if it's only for a few minutes."

"Yes. Ma'am. But, it's just like before. All gibberish to me."

"Go ahead, Audrey." Cadence reached for a pen and notepad.

"He said, 'Product forty-four pair'"

That would be the number of antlers harvested in the last week.

"Then, 'H-K plus plus.'"

The people in Hong Kong would take everything they could ship. "What's next?"

"'Rocky has an upside.'"

The hunters thought they could harvest more here in Rocky Mountain National Park. "Anything else?"

"He said, 'Willow lost.'"

"Say that again."

"'Willow lost.' I'm sure that's what he said. I asked him to repeat it twice. Is Willow a stock symbol or something?"

The pen clattered onto the desktop. "Yes, something like that."

"That's all, ma'am. And you know how sorry I am."

"I know, Audrey." As Cadence slammed the phone onto its hook, her fingernails found the scabs at her hairline and she began to pick at them.

Chapter Twelve

I flipped a sliver of steak off the edge of my paper plate. Zac caught it before it hit the deck.

"Don't say I never give you anything."

The dog tilted his head and yipped for more. I sent a second piece his way. He snapped it out of the air.

"You got me trained."

He barked again, and I answered with another chunk of the rib-eye. "That's all."

He growled.

"Okay, one more. But that's it." I dropped the last two scraps on the deck, folded the paper plate in half, laid it on the glowing coals in the firepan, and added another piece of split pine. I sat back in my chair and admired the skies over the valley. Zac curled up at my feet. Shadows stretched and the cool of night eased in around us. "Peaceful, isn't it, Zac?"

But saying it didn't make it so.

Anything close to peace stayed just beyond the images

of the drowned man in the stream and the sounds made when a bullet explodes window glass inches from a face. Even the raw stubs where someone had sawed away the bull elk's antlers threatened to fill my dreams. It was easier to quell those thoughts outside on the deck, away from the emptiness that cramped Jenny's cabin.

Vivid points of orange and red spiked the sky as the sun slipped behind the peaks. The day's warmth eased, and shades of gray cooled the evening air.

I fought to make it last a few seconds more.

Zac lifted his head, and a growl rumbled up from deep inside him.

"What is it, boy?"

At the end of our lane, where dirt met the asphalt, a vehicle turned toward my cabin. It rolled over the rutted gravel, its headlights twisting the aspens into strange shadows.

Zac trotted to the edge of the deck and his tail went still.

I recognized the truck. Click Batterton eased to a stop where the driveway ended and climbed out. He wore a battered Denver Broncos cap instead of his Smokey-the-Bear hat and a worn fleece vest and Levi's instead of the grays and greens of his Park Service uniform. He climbed the stairs and rubbed Zac's head when he reached the top.

"Hogan." He tipped his head.

"Hello, Click. Pull up a chair." I nodded at the only other one on the deck.

He settled into it, pulled Zac between his knees, and held the dog's face in his hands. "A lot of gray around his muzzle. How old is this dog getting to be?"

"He's coming up on fifteen."

"That's old for a beagle." He let Zac lick his fingers. "That's one thing the Almighty could have done better."

"What's that?"

"Dogs should live longer. You know, thirty, maybe thirty-five years." Batterton massaged Zac's ears. "That way, a man's first dog should teach him how to grow up. Then the next one to be there as he gets old." He patted Zac's head and ran his hands over the little hound's back. "Havin' two dogs in a lifetime would be about right. Losing a dog every ten years or so is too hard on a man."

Zac slumped onto his side and Batterton stroked his belly.

Batterton looked over at me. "Heard some rangers down at the visitor center talkin'. Said that kid pulled a big fish out of your secret beaver pond. That right?"

I nodded. "A big brookie. Every bit of fourteen inches." I leaned forward. "But you didn't come up here to talk about dogs and fish."

The ranger plucked a toothpick out from behind his ear and hung it in between his lips. "You were right about that elk. We found the bullet and sent it to the lab in Fort Collins. We'll know in the next few days if it matches the slug they found in your pickup. I'm guessing it won't." He moved the toothpick to the other side of his mouth. "I shouldn't be tellin' you any of this, Hogan, but you're knee deep in it . . ." He shifted in the chair so the shadows hid his face. "We got word out of Yellowstone and Grand Teton a couple of weeks ago. Seems poachers are workin' the parks up there, killin' bull elk and makin' off with the antlers. I guess they suspect the same bunch killed some elk in Glacier last month. They wanted us to keep up on our toes."

His eyes glowed like something wild in the firelight. "This ain't thrill killers shootin' just to see something die. Antlers still in velvet are worth more than a thousand bucks a pound in China and Japan and places like that. Rich old men over there grind 'em up into powder and put it in their tea. Claim it puts starch in their old peckers." He tossed his toothpick into the flames. "We're talkin' about big money to be made."

"This have something to do with who shot at me?"

He shrugged. "Could be. Maybe some poacher's workin' here. Saw you that morning and fired a shot to scare you off."

"Is that what you think?"

Batterton didn't answer. The pine logs on the fire hissed and popped. An ember flew on the deck and Batterton crushed it out with the toe of his boot. "I told you all I know. Everything else is just a guess."

"So, the drowned man wasn't as lucky as me?"

He shrugged. "We'd only be guessin'. And the wife's havin' the body shipped back to Iowa tomorrow."

"Find out anything from the autopsy?"

"Haven't released the results."

"And the woman I saw downtown with the wife?"

"Police chief is stayin' tight-lipped. I do know the driver's license she gave us was a fake. Willow—or whatever her name is—rented the car with a phony credit card. The rental company has filed a stolen car report. Every cop in the state is on the lookout for that red Corvette." He shook his head. "My boss told me to worry about the elk and keep my nose out of everything else. Like, I told you before, somethin' about this whole thing stinks."

"I think you're here to tell me something else."

Batterton nodded. "Don't shit in my park, Hogan." He stood from his chair and walked down the stairs to his truck. "Don't shit in my park.".

Chapter Thirteen

Cadence waited until after ten o'clock before she slipped down the back staircase into the hotel's lobby and crossed quickly to a phone booth. It was made of polished wood and had folding doors. She had played the good wife role, smiled, and said, "How quaint," almost every time they passed it. Her husband—her late husband—thought his appreciation of such things showed sophistication. Such things made her nauseous.

When she pulled the door shut, a tiny, bare light bulb flickered on and a fan hummed. She picked up the receiver, careful to keep her back to the crowd of guests at the registration desk, and dialed.

"Hello?"

"What do you mean Willow is lost?" she spit the words out.

"Hey, we agreed that we wouldn't call each other until things died down."

"And you agreed to keep a close watch on"—Cadence

fumbled for the right word—"the girl."

The line went silent.

"Well?" she hissed.

"I told you she was trouble. But you were feeling motherly. Weren't you, *Cadence?*" The voice drew out each syllable.

"Don't say my name."

More silence.

"Where is she?"

"She's just gone, *Cadence.*"

Her fingers found the faded scars at her hairline and she fought the urge to dig at them with her nails.

The voice on the other end of the line changed to a whisper. "We might have other problems. I think she took something."

Cadence felt the scabs tear away. "What?"

"There's money missing."

It made sense. Willow had guts. She never doubted that. "How much?"

"About everything we got from the Chinaman for the last shipment. I paid the hunters what they had coming. She took the rest."

Cadence did some quick calculations. Forty-four pairs of prime-still-in-velvet antlers. Maybe hundred fifty pounds per pair. Less the hunters cut. Willow had upwards of twenty-five thousand dollars. All of it in cash. She shifted in the cramped booth. "You fool."

"Listen, she can't have gone far. We'll find her. But I was thinking. It might be best for you not to be so close. Someone might, you know, make the connection."

"No. The difference between you and me is that even though we do the same things, you never know what you're doing. I plan for everything." She tapped the tip of one finger on the mouthpiece.

"Okay, okay. We'll find her."

"No, you'll find her." Cadence placed the receiver onto the cradle. She took a tissue from her purse and dabbed the tender places behind her ear.

Drops of fresh, red blood stained the Kleenex.

Chapter Fourteen

As the last bit of the day faded away, Zac curled up near my feet. Steel-colored, bulged-bottom clouds stacked along the mountain peaks, and faded stars speckled the sky. Somewhere up the valley a coyote yipped, and my dog raised his head to *wuff* a reply.

Jenny had chosen this place because of the night skies and the wildness. To me, it would always be her home.

The orange coals in the firepan dwindled to ashen-gray, and I pushed away the *what-might have-beens* and all of my *if-onlys*. I mulled over Batterton's last words. Were they a warning of some kind? Or a threat?

Before sleep found me, I decided where I would be in the morning.

—

I nosed Jenny's Volvo into a parking spot at the Lawn Lake Trailhead as dawn's first light spread over the valley. Two other cars sat side-by-side in the lot. Both had yellow placards taped to the inside of their windshields, showing that the backcountry campers had permission to park overnight.

A Winnebago sat by itself on the far side. There was no notice on its windows. Its occupants had most likely bucked the system, not willing to spend the five-dollar fee to stay in one of the park's campgrounds. If one of Batterton's Rangers found them, there'd be a ticket with a stiff fine.

Even on the July morning, wisps of steam showed in my breath as I made my way up from the valley floor. After a mile of switchbacks, I left the worn trail and bushwacked across the hillside toward the place I'd thought the gunshot must have come from. If I'd guessed right, it would be another mile and a half through the aspen to the spot above the river where the shooter had perched.

Dew-wet grass mashed under my boots. A dozen or more elk—cows with new calves—startled from their beds in the aspens and drifted like ghosts down the slope. In the morning air, their musky smell trailed behind them so thick I could taste it.

I picked my way through the shadowy woods. Golden sunbeams swept down through the aspen leaves, touching the ground like the tips of an artist's brush. Yellow turned to crimson in a single sparkle two steps in front of me.

A drop of blood clung to a bowing blade of grass. I studied the ground. One drop became two. Two, ten. In the next seconds of the new day's light, scarlet brush strokes painted the grasses. Drops turned to smears. Smears to wet blotches the size of dinner plates.

My guts clenched.

In the shadows of the lone pine in the grove of aspens, the breeze teased the pale belly hairs of an elk. Coaxed by the rising sun's brightness, gray shapes became clear. The elk's outstretched legs pointed up the hill. Its neck curved unnaturally down to the animal's head. The tongue lolled from its mouth in the animal's last gasp of life.

I backed away, listening for the sounds of a mountain lion slipping through the grasses. Sure, I had disturbed its kill before it had even begun to feed.

A tremble moved up my spine. I dug underneath my jacket for the folding knife on my belt.

My shoulders dropped when I turned back to the dead animal and a different fear took hold. No lion had laid in wait to spring and kill. A feather of steam rose from a quarter-sized puncture in the elk's ribs. Trails of dark red dripped from the place where someone had sawed away the bull's antlers. So much like the animal I found yesterday with Todd and his father. The kill was fresh. Flies hadn't yet found their way to the carcass.

The poachers Batterton told me about were hunting in the park. Maybe the one who had shot at me.

And maybe close by.

Over my head, pine needles danced in the breeze. Far below, a car passed on the road. I willed every muscle and fiber to be still. No twigs snapped under the foot of someone aiming a rifle to kill me. No leaves rustled as he stalked closer.

My knife would be useless against the gun the poacher had used to kill the elk. But I pulled it from the sheath and opened the blade.

Then hate replaced the fear. I hated the one who had killed the animal and left it here like so much garbage. The one who had so selfishly cut away the regal sweep of antlers. I darted across the hill, tossed myself over a fallen log, and hid in the shadows.

Time stretched like the sunlight finding its way to the hillside. My eyes strained, watching for movement.

Shiny black and brilliant white took shape in the shadows. Pulled by the scent of blood, a magpie glided through the trees. The bird lit on the stub of the dead elk's antler. It cocked its head like it was waiting for the creature to stir. Then its beak stabbed down into the beast's glassy eye. It lifted a morsel and gulped at its find.

In the next second, the bird froze, and then darted into the sky, a scrap falling from its beak. In a nearby tree, a pine squirrel scolded. I gripped the knife tighter. Up the hill, behind my back, boots scraped in the gravelly soil. I willed myself small.

"Don't move." A voice came down the slope. "We see you."

Sticky blood dripped from the stub of the elk's antler. The eye ruined by the bird stared at me.

Footfalls shuffled closer. "Stand up. Raise your hands."

I lifted myself back to the voice.

"Hands up where I can see 'em."

I spread my arms out like the figure on a cross, the knife still clutched in my fist.

"Drop the knife."

It slipped from my fingers and I sucked in a short breath.

"Now, turn around so I can see your face." Boots moved closer. "Slow. Do—everything—slow."

A fraction of an inch at a time, I moved my feet. Arms stretched wide from my sides. Stomach churning, lungs burning. Knowing I would die like the elk.

He wore the greens and browns of hunter's camouflage. Dark paint smudged his face. His rifle was at his shoulder, trained at me.

"Step out of those shadows so I can see you," the man ordered.

I focused on the barrel of his rifle, remembering the hole in the elk's ribs. My feet moved forward. Sunlight washed over my face, and in the glare, the gunman blurred.

From higher on the hill, another man moved closer to

the first. The brim of a black cowboy hat shaded his eyes. From his hip, the muzzle of a Winchester pointed at my stomach.

Chapter Fifteen

Cadence stared at the ceiling above her bed.

Willow had her money. And how much more did she know?

She tossed onto her side and smashed a fist into the pillow.

What if the girl was smarter than she'd given her credit? What if the money was just the beginning? What if Willow made a phone call to—

She twisted her grip on the pillow, wishing, in that instant, it was her daughter's throat, and squeezed.

Despite the cool mountain air, beads of sweat formed on her forehead and stung the raw scratched places at her hairline.

Just after dawn, she crept down the stairs to the phone booth in the empty lobby. She dialed the local number she had memorized. The phone rang a dozen times before she slammed it down.

"Ms. Tait?" A man in the dark blue bellhop uniform

tapped on the glass. "Is everything all right?"

Cadence shook her head. *Must keep up the act.* She dabbed at her eyes with a crumpled tissue.

She inched the booth's door open. "I'm fine." Then, "No, I'm not." She turned from the bellhop. "I thought of something that must be included in my husband's service. A song. His favorite song." She touched the tissue to her lips and supped up a deep breath. "But our minister isn't answering."

"Ms. Tait, I could get you some coffee if you'd like."

"That would be fine." She looked down at the Kleenex. Smeared lipstick blended with dried drops of her blood. "Cream and two sugars," she told the employee. She dialed the number again and waited for her brother to answer.

Chapter Sixteen

I swallowed hard and stared at the muzzles of the guns pointed at me.

"Hogan?" The voice was Batterton's. He spit the words at me. "I told you to stay out of this."

My eyes shut in relief. I dropped my arms.

"Hands up." The painted-face gunman made a quick upward gesture with the muzzle of his rifle.

I lifted my arms again and stepped from the glaring sun into a spot of shade.

"Don't be a fool, Taylor. That's Hogan." Batterton pushed his cowboy hat back on his head and moved toward me.

"Maybe he's one of the poachers, sir."

Behind the paint, I could see Ranger-boy's face. He dipped his head toward the dead animal.

"Hogan didn't shoot no elk." More irritation than anger filled Batterton's voice.

Ranger-boy's rifle was still pointed at me.

"And Taylor, you fool. Before you point your gun at somebody, you identify yourself as Park Service law enforcement. You were lucky this time. You might not be next time if there is a next time." He spit tobacco on the ground. "Besides, if anybody's gonna shoot Hogan's ass off, it's gonna be *me*."

Batterton pulled off his hat and dabbed his forehead with his shirtsleeve. "Answer me, Hogan. What in the hell gave you the right to go and play frickin' John Wayne in my Park?" He wiped a brown dribble from the corner of his mouth.

Cool air filled my lungs. "Can I put my hands down now?"

"Yeah, put 'em down." Batterton rested his rifle over his shoulder. He turned to Ranger-boy. "Don't shoot him when he does, Taylor." Then to me, "If it wasn't for all the paperwork there'd be, I just might let him."

My arms dropped, and I flexed my fingers. "What's going on here?"

"No, Hogan. Uh-uh. It's me that asks the questions. Like, what the hell are *you* doing up here?"

"I wanted to see the place, um . . . where whoever shot at me."

"I figured as much." The Ranger shook his head.

I nodded toward the elk. "The poachers you told me about?"

"Yup. Taylor found another dead bull elk up on top of the hill. I'm guessin' that one fell where they shot it." Batterton moved closer to the one I'd found and hunkered down on his heels. "Shot this one a little too far back." He tapped the hole in its ribs with the barrel of his rifle. "Lung shot. Didn't go right down. We were following the blood trail when we spotted you. They sawed the antlers off the one up above just like here." Batterton reached out and gently laid his hand on the animal's muzzle. "Still warm.

Ain't been dead no more than a half hour. Hear a shot?"

I shook my head.

"Figures." Batterton stood up. He took a red kerchief from his pocket and tied it to a limb of the tree above where the elk lay. "These bad-asses know what they're doin'."

"Sir?" Ranger-boy spoke for the first time since he'd ordered me to raise my hands. "Should you tell him any of this?"

"Hogan got himself in the middle. He's got a right to know."

"But, sir—"

"Hogan won't say anything." He looked me in the eye. "Will you?"

I sucked my bottom lip over my teeth and shook my head.

"When I told you that we had word on poachers working in Yellowstone, I didn't tell you the whole story. Last weekend, dead elk started turning up on the Grand Lake side of the Park. Close to a dozen. All mature bulls. Antlers sawed off every one of 'em. Then hikers found two, not a mile from the east entrance." He fanned his face with his hat. "While they were lookin' around the area where you got shot at yesterday, Taylor spotted another bull down across the river. 'Bout a quarter mile from where you found that dead man in the river." He looked at me but raised his voice. "Taylor's got the makin's of a good Ranger if he don't shoot some tourist first."

Taylor lowered his eyes and stared at the ground.

Batterton went on. "The one you found by your beaver pond and these two make six on this side of the Park. How many more we haven't found is anybody's guess." He shook his head.

"But, sir," Ranger-boy said. "We didn't hear any shot and Hogan didn't either. You think they're using a rifle with a silencer?"

Batterton nodded.

"I bet there's two of them," the kid said. "We thought they were killing the animal and coming back later to get the antlers. These were cut off almost as soon as the elk hit the ground. I'll bet they're hunting as a team."

"Maybe he's right," I said. "Take two to carry the antlers off this hill."

"Yeah, maybe." Batterton chased a fly from his face with his hand.

"When they shot at me, I heard the shot."

"I read in *Guns and Ammo* that a silencer can affect accuracy," the kid volunteered

"Yeah," It made sense to me. "Or he might have taken the silencer off because he wanted me to hear. Scarin' me was all that mattered."

"And that's why he only shot one time," the kid nodded.

Batterton jammed his hat back on his head. "Anything else?"

"Winnebago." I turned toward the trailhead where I'd parked Jenny's car. "Before they shot at me yesterday, a Winnebago passed me. This morning when I parked my car, there was a Winnebago in the parking lot at the Lawn Lake trailhead." Remembering the puff of exhaust. "Older Winnebago. I think it was the same one. You got to let someone know."

"Taylor, get on the radio and tell headquarters to get someone to the Lawn Lake parking area."

Ranger-boy dug into the cargo pocket on his pant leg. He pulled out the walkie-talkie, flipped a switch, and said into the box, "Eagle's Nest, this is Falcon Eyes, copy?"

Batterton shook his head. "Them pup-Rangers watch too much television."

—

As Taylor fiddled with the radio, Batterton explained that

after he left my cabin last night, he joined teams from the Park Service, the State Division of Wildlife, and U.S. Game and Fish to patrol the park and watch for any sign of the poachers. He and Taylor volunteered for the hill above Horseshoe Park and Fall River. They'd spent the night on the hillside and were about to head in when Taylor found the first dead elk and the blood trail that had led them to me.

Taylor looked down at the radio in his hands, twisted a dial, and lifted the device to his ear. "Say again," he spoke into the microphone. "Ten-four, *I think*." He shook his head and turned to Batterton. "They said for us to hurry down to the trailhead." The paint had smudged around his mouth, turning his lips green. "And, sir, they have someone in custody."

Batterton's tongue drew a slow circle on the inside of his cheek. "They say who?"

Ranger-boy shook his head. "No, sir. It was hard to hear because of the static and all, but they want us to hurry down there and I think they said, to watch the treetops"— his face twisted with confusion "—for *antlers*."

—

Below us, a park ranger stood with his back to the open door of the Winnebago. Where a fringe of white and yellow wildflowers surrounded a picnic table, a second ranger perched the butt stock of a short-barreled shotgun on his hip and kept watch on a man seated on the table's bench.

The man's back rested against the edge of the table. His arms hung in the space between the tabletop and the seat. As he shifted, sunlight flashed off the chrome handcuffs around his wrists.

"Appears you might be right about that Winnebago, Hogan."

Batterton and I paused where the trees gave way to the

meadow above the trailhead. The old Ranger put his rifle over his shoulder and marched down the hill.

Behind us, Ranger-boy zigzagged through the aspen groves. Each time I glanced back, his head was up, scanning the trees like the voice on the walkie-talkie had ordered.

Two green park service pickups and a white one with the U.S. Fish and Wildlife emblem on its door lined the center of the narrow strip of asphalt, blocking the backpackers' cars and my Volvo from any chance of leaving. I hurried to keep up with Batterton.

A woman in Levi's and a park service green nylon jacket stepped from the door of the Winnebago. She combed her wind-whipped black hair away from her face with her hand. A man in starched and creased camos followed her from the coach. He shut the door behind him.

"That's my new boss, Phoebe American Horse." Batterton paused at the parked cars. "Been here less than three months. Head law enforcement ranger for the whole park. They tell me she's real smart. I just don't know how clever she is. Sometimes smart isn't enough to catch poachers." He dribbled a stream of tobacco juice onto the ground.

The man in the fresh camo fatigues went to the white pickup, reached inside, and snaked the cord of a radio handset to his mouth. He turned his back and began to talk.

"That's Tucker. Headman with Federal Fish and Wildlife around here." Batterton tipped his head toward the white truck. "If he thinks he's gonna be the one that gets credit for any of this, he's underestimatin' American Horse. This kinda thing has *high profile* written all over it. Word is she's the kind that has no problem steppin' on toes to get to the front of the line." He jammed his hands into his jacket pockets. "Crap, here she comes. Let me do the talkin'."

The Native American woman walked around the end of Jenny's car and met us. From a distance, her hair had looked midnight black. Up close, threads of silver interlaced the black and sparkled in the sun. Her face was narrow, with high cheekbones, and vestiges of old acne peeked from behind a layer of makeup. She eyed Batterton and then me. "*Who* are you?"

Batterton spoke before I could. "This is Guy Hogan, boss. A friend of mine. Just happened to be out hiking this morning and ran into us."

She shook her head so slightly that it barely moved. "Bullshit."

Batterton rubbed his chin.

"I read your report about the gunshot yesterday morning," she said.

It was my turn. "I wanted to see if I could find any evidence on the hill about the one who shot at me. Batterton didn't know anything about my plans." American Horse coolly appraised each word I said. "In fact, last night he told me to stay away. I didn't listen."

Batterton straightened his shoulders and cut in. "Hogan found a dead bull elk on the hillside. Taylor and me found another up above. Both fresh-killed. It was Hogan that told us he remembered seein' the Winnebago before he got shot at yesterday. Then he saw it again when he parked here this morning. That's why we radioed in."

When Batterton mentioned the motor home, the man at the picnic table turned for a better look at us. His face was as round as a new nickel. A week's worth of dark stubble covered his cheeks. Over one eye, a shiny pink scar peeked out from under his greasy hair. Perhaps yesterday morning, he had looked at me through the sights on his rifle.

Then Batterton nodded toward the man at the picnic table. "Whatcha got on him?"

American Horse's eyes gave me the lecture about not getting involved in her business. When she spoke, I was sure I wasn't supposed to listen. I stepped back and listened, anyway.

"Ranger Stalls got your message,"—she caught a loose strand of hair and tucked it behind her ear—"and made for the trailhead. He saw that man coming out of the aspens, and he had blood on his shirt and pants. He detained him and sent for us. The door of the Winnebago was open when we got here. We asked permission to search. The detainee refused to speak. When I looked inside, I saw a box of rifle ammunition on a table. *In plain view.*" She was careful to emphasize those words. "We stepped inside to see what else we might find."

"Any sign of a rifle or the antlers?"

"She shook her head and went on. "We know from the VIN number that the coach was purchased in Longmont last month. And the license plates are stolen. Tucker is on the radio trying to get a search warrant now."

"Batterton—" Ranger-boy's voice floated down the hill. "You might want to see this."

Phoebe American Horse moved up the hill. I wondered for a second if I should go with them and then followed Batterton.

—

Sweat lines cut the camouflage paint on Ranger-boy's face. He stood in a splash of sunlight where an aspen grove met a cluster of Ponderosa Pines. When he saw us, he pointed at the ground near the base of the biggest pine.

"What is it?" American Horse asked. Batterton and I panted for breath after the run up the hill. She didn't.

"Blood." Ranger-boy knelt and touched the ground near a red splotch he could have covered with a coffee mug. "I saw this and was sure that there was another dead elk close." His fingers clawed at a gnat stuck in the sticky paint on his upper lip. "I looked all around, then remembered what he said about the trees and looked"—he tilted his head back, stood and pointed—"up there. See it?"

Wrapped in brown burlap, a bundle hung from a branch a long arm's length above the boy's head. Flies buzzed around the top of the package. I squinted to see more. What looked like wrapped tree branches became the antlers of a five-point bull elk. The fuzzy velvet covering that protected the new antler bulged where strips of twine held the burlap. My mind attached those antlers to the bloody stumps of the elk I'd found on the hill, and my stomach turned over in disgust.

"Good job, Taylor," American Horse said and then turned to us. "A tourist came into Park headquarters late yesterday with a bundle just like it. When he took us out to where he found it, there was a dead elk a hundred yards away. That's why we sent word to look in the trees around any new kills."

Taylor stretched to take the bundle.

She grabbed his arm. "Leave it there. I want pictures."

"Stalls will have a camera in his truck," Batterton said. "I'll go get him."

"No, I've sent for the sheriff's crime lab." She wanted the control. "I want everything documented properly. The park wrangler is on the way with mules. As soon as they get here, you and Taylor will go with him and bring down the elk you found." She turned to Ranger-boy. "Stay here and see to it that nothing is disturbed." With that, she strode off down the hill.

—

By the time Batterton and I made it to the trailhead, a sheriff's car, a station wagon with park service markings, and a mud-splattered pickup from the Colorado Division of Wildlife added to the line of cars around the Winnebago. A curl of smoke rose from a cigarette in the lips of the little man seated at the picnic table, but his hands were still fastened behind him.

Batterton eyed the maze of vehicles. "Looks like you're gonna be here awhile." He nodded to where American Horse stood with a gray-haired man in a silver-belly Stetson. "That's Dalton Cummings. DOW officer 'round here. You know him?"

"Heard a lot about him, but I've never met him."

"We'll wait 'til he's through with her and I'll introduce you. He's put up with this kind of rodeo before, and I'll bet he's got a thermos of hot coffee in his truck. I could sure use a cup."

I remembered I hadn't eaten since the steak I'd shared with Zac. My stomach rolled over.

A sheriff's deputy stepped up and touched American Horse's arm. He jerked his thumb over his shoulder. A van marked Larimer County Crime Lab eased into the line of parked cars. They left Cummings and went to the van.

Cummings crossed to the picnic table, hunkered down on his heels in front of the man in handcuffs, and asked him something. The man shrugged. Cummings shook his head, stood, and walked to where we waited.

"We're too old for this, Dalton." Batterton reached out his hand and Cummings took it.

"If it wasn't so much fun, I'd be retired." The game warden winked and held out his hand toward me.

"Dalton, meet Guy Hogan."

"You the fella that got shot at yesterday?" Cummings took my hand with a firm grip.

"Yup." Guessing that the bullet that shattered my windshield had given me celebrity status I didn't want.

"You might as well be here. Seems everybody else is." Cummings shook his head at the cluster of cars in the parking lot. "Hear you boys found some dead elk on the hill?"

"Yeah, with their antlers sawed off," I answered. "You know that man?" I pointed at the picnic table.

"Hayden Bumpus. I doubt there's a game warden in this part of the state that hasn't had a run-in with him or his brother. That's one blood-thirsty son-of-a-bitch, for sure. 'Bout three years ago, I caught 'em both spotlightin' deer just outside of Loveland. They'd shot a doe with twin fawns. When the little ones nuzzled their dead mother, the sons-of-bitches shot 'em with their mouths still on her tits." He huffed in disgust. "Hauled 'em in, confiscated their truck and guns. The next week, heard they were at it again up Wyoming way." He unbuttoned his shirt cuffs and rolled the sleeves up to his elbows. "He's just sittin' there. Won't say a word. But I'll tell ya, I got no doubt he's up to his eyeballs in all this. But neither him nor his brother is smart enough to pull this off on their own. This many elk antlers is high dollars. Somebody smarter put 'em up to it."

"You tell that to American Horse?" Batterton asked.

"She didn't want to listen."

Both men shook their heads.

Finally, Cummings spoke. "You boys need some coffee?"

Chapter Seventeen

Willow had planned to ditch the Corvette in Frisco or Glenwood Springs or Grand Junction, buy a bus ticket, and head west to Salt Lake City. Then a plane ticket to Phoenix or San Diego. From there, the next stop could be Mexico. A girlfriend had promised her a job slinging top-shelf cocktails to moneyed, fat couples at a beachside resort.

She'd work out the details as she needed. The one part of her plan she was sure of was to never talk to her mother again.

Two things changed the plan.

The knapsack she'd snatched from the cabinet in her uncle's dingy kitchen was stuffed with more cash than she expected. And he had told her there was more coming. More was always better.

The other was the lead story on every top-of-the-hour radio news broadcast since she had left Estes Park. Paxton Tait—Iowa businessman and senate appointee—

had drowned in Rocky Mountain National Park. Willow's hands tightened on the steering wheel. Willow knew it could be no coincidence that her mother arranged for her to drive by the very spot where Paxton Tait had drowned. And no accident Willow had been there at the time when the body was found. Her mother enjoyed the details. Especially when the details made her daughter squirm.

Willow thought over the time in the bar in Estes Park. Cadence had not said one word about her husband when they met for drinks.

Was it just another of her mother's cruel ways or part of some bigger plan?

Certainly not motherly love.

Rage built. Willow hurled an empty coffee cup across the car.

No doubt, her mother was adding up her share of the life insurance money now. She'd probably called a realtor to list the family mansion before she'd called the mortician.

From what Willow had learned from her uncle, this elk antler thing was bigger than she thought. Add to it the money her mother would split with Paxton's adult children, and Cadence Tait was planning a big score.

But Willow had other things to consider. She forced herself to calm down. To think things through the details. Like her mother would.

The Corvette was over seventy-two hours past due to the rental company. If the police weren't looking for it by now, they would be soon. Her uncle was right about one thing. The car stuck out like a sore thumb.

She took the Vail exit from Interstate 70. Summer vacationers would be leaving the highway at dark for hotels and campgrounds. The Corvette would be too easy to spot in the lighter evening traffic.

Cadence's husband's death had slipped to the third on the evening radio update—behind a new quarterback signing by the Denver Broncos and four traffic fatalities. There had been no mention of the elk poaching on any of the dozen radio stations she scanned since leaving Estes Park.

She followed a shiny new Bentley into a hotel parking garage on Vail's main street. She counted two Porches and three Mercedes in the garage. But it was a red Corvette with Texas license plates that gave her an idea.

She found a place for her Corvette on the third level. The elevator from the parking structure opened into an airy lobby with views of the ski slopes. Guests headed for a day of shopping brushed by her and a steel-haired man with sunglasses that cost as much as a new Cadillac pretended to adjust his tennis sweater as he studied her tight jeans.

Vail was not at all like Estes Park. It made her smile.

The man behind the registration desk tugged at the collar of a too-big uniform shirt and asked, "Reservations, ma'am?"

Willow gathered her thick, blond hair with both hands and pulled it into a ponytail, careful to be sure that her tank top pulled tight over her breasts. "I stayed with you last winter and enjoyed it so much." Her eyes found the brass nameplate on his shirt. "You do have something available, don't you, Tony?"

Tony frowned and looked down at the registry on the desk in front of him. "We've been quite busy."

Willow leaned forward. "Oh, please," she purred, "you were such a help last winter, Tony. It was you I remember, wasn't it?"

"I do have a suite on the concierge floor. One ninety-nine plus—"

"I'll take it." She had moved a bundle of one-hundred-dollar bills from her uncle's knapsack into her purse. She slipped three of them across the counter.

"I'll need some form of identification."

"Is that necessary?" she added another hundred-dollar bill to the stack.

The man covered the money with his hand. "I understand." He nodded. "Should I call a bellman to help with your luggage?"

"I think not."

He placed a room key on the counter. "If you need anything—"

"I'll be sure to ask for you, Tony." She let her fingers graze the back of his hand.

Willow crossed the lobby. She paused to fill a cup with coffee. When Tony turned his back and slipped the money into his trousers' pocket, Willow plucked a black cap with Vail spelled out in glittery letters from a display in the hotel gift shop. The price tag showed $29.95. Without looking back, she put it into her purse.

—

The room was on the twelfth floor, facing the manicured ski runs, now lush with summer grass and wildflowers. A king-sized bed in the sleeping room was positioned where guests could see the mountainside without so much as lifting their heads from the pillows. A sunken, jetted tub in the marble-floor bath shared the same view. Willow wriggled out of her tight jeans and took a bottle of chardonnay from the mini-fridge. She'd taken a deep breath, snatched the backpack she had taken from her uncle's cabin, and let the cash tumble onto the bed.

The backpack was green nylon and a National Park Service emblem was embroidered on the top flap. There were two more bundles of hundred-dollar bills—in addition to the one she'd used to pay for the hotel room. The crisp, new hundreds were bundled in stacks of fifty bills. Three bundles. Fifteen thousand dollars. Less what she gave to

Tony. The rest of the money was loose. Fifties. Twenties and tens. A few fives and ones.

Willow separated the bills by the president picture and arranged them in mounds, not neat stacks, along the foot of the king-sized bed, making sure each pile barely touched the next.

Willow opened a second bottle of wine. She peeled off her tank top, stretched out on the bed, and clutched an unopened bundle of hundreds in each hand. Her thumbs fanned the crisp new bills like playing cards. She thought of her mother, and then, like she wanted to do so often, she stuck out her tongue and let her bare feet play in the heaps of loose money.

Chapter Eighteen

Dalton Cummings splashed coffee from a stainless-steel thermos into Styrofoam cups. The deputies and rangers that gathered around his truck's tailgate wore scuffed work boots and pants with threadbare knees. The men with polished shoes and creases in their jeans stood across the lot with American Horse. Ranger-boy left that group and came to stand beside Batterton.

"She thinks she's a general fixin' to invade another country, and she's lovin' every minute of it." The game warden took a coffee can from the toolbox behind his truck's cab, popped the lid off, and handed the can to Taylor. "Take a couple and pass that around. Ginger snaps. My wife made 'em. Tried chocolate chip, but they melt into a big lump. Same with peanut butter. Oatmeal dries out, but ginger snaps can ride around in a pickup for a month and still taste good." His eyes sparkled. "Be careful, you don't break a tooth."

Batterton took the can from Ranger-boy and popped a

cookie into his mouth. "I'm bettin' this batch is two months old, Dalton," he mumbled between bites.

Around the truck, men laughed but took the cookies when their turn came.

"This here shindig reminds me of the fella who felt the call of nature, so's he went out back to use the outhouse." Cummings paused and motioned with the thermos to see who needed more coffee. "That outhouse was an old two-holer and one of the seats was already taken. But that Mexican food he'd had for dinner was beginnin' to percolate, so he sat on down."

Cummings waited until everyone looked his way. "Anyways, the other fella finished his business, stood up, and as he was pullin' up his britches, a quarter fell out of his pocket and dropped right down that outhouse hole." The game warden tugged at the end of his drooping white mustache. "That fella took a look down the hole, shrugged his shoulders, and buckled up his Levis. Then he fished out his billfold, found a new twenty-dollar bill, folded it in two, and dropped it down the hole." The men around the truck leaned forward. "'Why'd you do that?' the first ole boy asked him. The fella looked at him and said, 'You don't think I'm goin' down there for a quarter, do ya?'"

Deep laughter filled the air and echoed back from the hillside.

Dalton gestured at the parking lot full of cars. "I'm tellin' ya, I've worked for the government my whole life, but when it comes to something like this here. They'll spend twenty dollars on what two-bits can fix and be proud of theirselves while they're doin' it," he said just loud enough for those close to him to hear.

American Horse stepped away from her circle of followers. She nodded to a Ray-Banned and pressed-trousered deputy sheriff. The deputy walked to Hayden Bumpus, still on the picnic table bench. He plucked the cigarette stub from the handcuffed man's lips and pulled him to his feet.

Bumpus fought the deputy's grip and turned his moon face to look our way. From behind his back, he raised his cuffed hands just enough to point a bony finger toward the group—but I could swear he pointed it only at me—and he snapped his thumb forward. The deputy pulled him away and pushed him into the back seat of his car.

"Shit fire," Cummings whistled through his teeth. "What do you make of that?"

Batterton stepped in so that he blocked my view of Bumpus. "He must have heard us talkin' about Hogan seein' the Winnebago."

Cummings dumped his coffee on the ground. "He's a mean one. And his brother, Tommy, is meaner still. You watch yourself, Hogan."

Batterton waited for the patrol car to pull away. "He's right. That sumbitch knows how to work the system. He'll call his lawyer and is liable to post bail and be out by tonight. You might wanna think about getting outta Estes for a few days, Hogan." The lawmen around the truck shook their heads.

I nodded, not quite sure if it was fear that filled me or the revenge I wanted for the elk he killed.

"You got a pistol at home, doncha?" Cummings asked.

"Yeah."

"You be sure it's loaded."

Chapter Nineteen

Cadence Tait tapped the legal pad in her lap with the pen and slowly reread what she had written. She scribbled "touch eyes" in the margin near the top of the page and further down added "gesture to rangers". She closed her eyes and imagined the tomorrow afternoon's scene.

Television cameras would be trained on her. Microphones in the hands of reporters pressed closer to where she would be standing. The mountains behind her. Surrounded by uniformed rangers and police. One of the reporters—one of those national networks, handsome, just-out-of-college types—would say softly into his microphone, "Despite her loss, how beautiful and strong Cadence appeared."

Beautiful and strong

He'd left out one thing. *Rich.* Cadence was beautiful and strong and things were coming together to make her very rich.

She moved across the hotel room, laid the tablet on the

dresser, and read the script out loud. At just the right place, she touched her eyes, as if to catch a tear. As she practiced the final words of thanks, Cadence raised her hand to the rangers she imagined would be standing nearby.

She checked her watch. Two minutes.

Good. Anything longer would be edited in the TV newsrooms.

The phone on the dresser rang. Cadence waited until the third ring before picking it up.

"Hello."

"Ms. Tait, Mike Sanchez, here."

"How can I help you, Mike?"

"I just got off the phone with the coroner. He's agreed to release your husband's body. The cause of death will be listed as accidental drowning. Like we talked about at the hospital. Since there were no witnesses, he's reserving the right to reopen the investigation if he deems it appropriate later on. Standard procedure, like we talked about. Any questions?"

"No." Cadence studied herself in the mirror above the dresser. On her cheek, near her lips, an ugly red spot marred her near-perfect skin. She touched it. A pimple?

"Ms. Tait? Any questions."

She leaned closer to the mirror. "No. Let the hospital know my attorney will be in touch in the morning to make the final arrangements."

"Once again, ma'am. I'm very sorry for your loss. Is there anything I or my people can do?"

"You know, Mike,"–Cadence touched the red mark again—"Paxton's friends from Iowa have scheduled a press conference at Park headquarters tomorrow afternoon. I want to formally thank the rangers and the people at the hospital for all they've done. I'd like you to be there, of course. And bring some of your officers. It's scheduled for six tomorrow evening." She pursed her lips to tighten the skin near the blemish.

Not a pimple. A mosquito bite. Damn the insects.

She would need a bit more concealer tomorrow.

She wouldn't want all those watching on television to think she had a pimple.

Chapter Twenty

Willow woke with a dull headache from too much wine. Evening skies touched the mountain tops and the lights along Vail's cobblestone walking mall flickered. Tourists filled the tables of the trendy restaurants along the street side. She lifted several fifty-dollar bills from the bed with her toes and let them flutter to the floor.

Restaurants she could now afford.

She dressed in the same tight jeans. She selected a favorite blouse from her suitcase and freshened her lipstick. Rather than spend too much time on her hair, she combed it and perched the cap she had taken from the giftshop on her head.

She took ten of the hundred-dollar bills from the open bundle, stuffed them into the back pocket of her jeans, and jammed the rest of the money back into the backpack. Tucked into the knapsack's front pocket, she discovered a small black leather-covered journal—the kind that held clues for the detectives in black and white movies from the

1950s. The thrill of what she might have teased her.

Dinner would have to wait.

Willow sat on the edge of the bed and began to read. Each page was more interesting than the one before.

Lists of the number of antlers harvested filled most of the first third of the book. Besides Colorado, there were tallies for Montana, Idaho, and Wyoming. Next, she found pages of names, identifying hunters, drivers, buyers, or exporters, and each categorized by state and number of transactions. All transactions were made in cash. Final tabulations showed more than a quarter million dollars.

She glanced at the backpack on the bed. What Willow had counted was only a pittance of what had been collected so far. She remembered what her uncle had told her.

More money was on its way.

That was why her mother was in Colorado in person.

Willow found that calmness her mother was so good at and forced herself to slow down. She began at the first page again. When she had finished, she thumbed back through the list of names. On the Colorado list, she found a name she recognized. *Usher.* The man she had met at her uncle's. But it was the side note that interested her most.

Scribbled in the margin: *Watch him!! Cunt hound!!*

She hated the word, but recalled the way his cool eyes had appraised her tight jeans. Usher's address was listed in Grand Lake. There was a phone number, too.

She finished her next chardonnay before she finished her third reading of the notebook. What she read, she enjoyed much more than the wine.

—

At two a.m., Willow crept back to the parking garage. Instead of boots with leather soles and heels, she wore tennis shoes. Her hair was pulled back and tucked into the hood of a navy-blue sweatshirt. She found the car she had spotted earlier on the parking structure's fourth floor.

The new red Corvette had Texas license plates. With the stubby screwdriver she always kept in her purse, she traded the plates from the Texas car with the plates from her overdue rental. Police on the lookout for the missing Corvette were sure to check the license plates before pulling the car over.

Most times, the simplest diversion was the best. Her mother had taught her that.

While climbing the back stairs to her room, Willow imagined the Texas couple charming their neighbors at their next backyard cocktail party with stories of their involvement in criminal mischief.

Chapter Twenty-One

Fatigue pushed me into a spot of shade at the same picnic table where Hayden Bumpus had been handcuffed. Images of dead elk and Bumpus's thumb snapping forward on his pointed finger sat there with me.

Cummings's ginger snaps swam in the coffee I'd poured into my stomach. The concoction boiled, its fumes crawled up my throat and settled into a warm spot behind my sternum.

Official vehicles still blocked Jenny's Volvo. With nowhere to go, I settled in and watched American Horse command her troops.

Batterton left Ranger-boy with the wrangler and crossed to where I waited. "Word came they found the second set of antlers." Batterton propped one foot onto the bench. "Just like the other. Wrapped in burlap. Hung in a tree. You and me must have walked within twenty feet of 'em." He shooed a fly that hovered near his mouth. "That put a smile on American Horse's face."

"Any sign of a rifle?"

"They went through the motorhome and didn't find nothin'. She's got a team combin' the hillside to see if he hid it up there. If they don't find a gun, it'll be tough makin' any charges stick. All they have for sure is the blood on his shirt. A good lawyer will say Bumpus was off on a hike and found the elk like we did." Batterton tucked a pinch of Skoal into the side of his cheek.

"Maybe he hung the rifle in the tree like the antlers," I asked him.

"She thought of that. Tomorrow morning there's gonna be a whole passel of rangers with stiff necks from looking up at treetops." He forced a smile that didn't last.

"Too many things don't add up," I told him.

"Like?"

"Your new boss said that the first ranger found the Winnebago with the door open. It wasn't opened when I pulled in here. I think I'd remember that." I watched Batterton rolling the chew in his mouth. "Remember what we talked about up on the hill? A team. Two men. One man did the shooting. The other cut the antlers off. Cummings said there were two brothers."

"And?"

"What if the other brother, Tommy, I think he called him, hurried off the hill to stash the rifle in the Winnebago, while his brother's still on the hill hid the antlers?" I let my thoughts come. "He hears Stalls' truck and takes off. Stalls doesn't see the first brother, but sees Hayden coming out of the trees with the blood on his shirt. Puts him in handcuffs." I looked up at Batterton. "So, where did the other brother go?"

He raised his eyes and gazed over my head and across the road.

I knew what he was looking at. I'd fished in Fall River Valley too many times to count. The river wound its way through the marsh about four hundred yards from us. On this side, willow bushes crowded a swampy meadow. The ground turned firm on the other side of the river. Aspens grew thick on the valley floor and blended into a stand of dark pines that covered the steep, north-facing slope.

"Someone hidin' over there would be tough to spot, even if you knew where to look."

Batterton made a bulge in his cheek with the wad of tobacco. "So, Tommy Bumpus is hidin' over there?"

"Not now. He'd take off when he saw all the activity over here. It'd be a hard haul, but at the top of the hill he'd find —"

"Trail Ridge Road." Batterton looked over my shoulder at the far hillside.

My mind traced a path through the timber to the road on top. "Should we tell American Horse?"

"She's more worried about a TV crew that's supposed to be on its way." He dribbled brown juice onto the ground. "And I've been ordered to go retrieve the dead elk." He tipped his head toward Ranger-boy and the mules. The young Ranger held the halters on a pair of mules while the wrangler strapped pack saddles to their backs. "I told you before. Let us do our jobs. American Horse won't like you pokin' around."

"I don't answer to her. She can't stop me from walking over there and lookin' around."

"What if she asks what you're doin'? What you gonna tell her?"

"That I had to take a leak. Old man's bladder and all that coffee, you know."

He moved the tobacco to the other side of his mouth. "You're gonna do what you want, aren't you, Hogan?" He turned to walk away way and stopped. "Dalton was serious about you keepin' a gun handy. The police can only do so much."

The warm spot in my chest turned hot. I nodded.

Batterton and Ranger-boy started up the hill with the wrangler and his mules before I stood. Dalton Cummings's DOW pickup rumbled by on the road back to town. The old man raised a finger from the steering wheel as he passed me.

I tried to imagine which way I'd go if it was me, hurrying away from the dead elk on the hill. My head told me that the man with the gun, if there was one, would have tried to stay in the trees rather than take the shorter route across the open meadow. I gritted my teeth and started for the other side of the road.

American Horse's voice stopped me. "Mister Hogan?" She stepped out from between the trucks that blocked Jenny's Volvo.

"I'm going to have someone to move these cars so you can be on your way." She watched Batterton and the mules over my shoulder. "We're expecting a tow truck any time now. They'll need room to maneuver, so we'll want all these cars out of here."

I looked across the meadow.

She moved closer. "I'm not going to say anything about what you tried to do on your own. I'll assume you've learned your lesson and that you will let the proper authorities do their job."

Loop earrings made of multicolored beads swung from her earlobes. She was older than I first thought. Maybe my age. Fine creases lined the skin along her jaw and vestiges of old acne pocked her cheeks. Still, Phoebe American Horse was a handsome woman.

"Do we understand each other?" she asked.

I took a quick look back at the meadow.

"Mister Hogan?"

"I understand."

"May I ask you something else?" She tilted her head.

I nodded.

"How well do you know Batterton?"

"Fly fishing mostly. He checked my license a couple of times. We hit it off. He recommended a couple of places to fish and it was him that got me guiding for one of the fly shops in town. Why?"

"No reason." She studied my face, and I waited for another question, but it didn't come.

Over the top of her head, I saw another ranger with a man and a woman. Sleeping bags were strapped to the top of the couple's backpacks. They wore hiking boots and the dirt and sweat from time in the backcountry. The man pointed at a car parked next to Jenny's. The ranger motioned for them to stay where they were and he came to American Horse.

"Ma'am," he said as he stepped up, "backpackers from one of those cars. They're anxious to leave."

"I need to ask them if they saw anything. Then they can be on their way." American Horse looked back at me. "Mister Hogan is anxious to be going, also."

The ranger shuffled his feet. "Ma'am, they also said that there's a lot of water leaking through the old dam at Lawn Lake. They think someone should go up there and take a look."

I heard a car coming our way. American Horse turned toward the sound. A big number nine was painted on the side of a four-wheel drive from a TV station in Denver. A smile spread over her face. She looked at the backpackers and then the Ranger. "I don't have time for that now." She glanced at the news team climbing from their car. "Tell them 'thank you' and we'll have someone look into it."

—

I tightened my sore fingers over the steering wheel. When I saw my eyes in the rearview mirror, they were years older than yesterday. Jenny said that we would age together in our home in these mountains. Without her, I would grow old alone.

I followed the backpacker's car to the main road. They turned towards the town. I paused at the stop sign and eyed the north slope above the valley. Even if I headed up to Trail Ridge, what could I expect to find? Tommy Bumpus with a rifle on his shoulder waiting beside the road?

The heartburn in my chest needed food to chase away the heat. Dark clouds hung over the mountaintops, and a slash of lightning stabbed the highest point on Longs Peak.

I turned toward home, and the heartburn turned to fire.

Chapter Twenty-Two

plucked the local newspaper from the mailbox and met Zac at the front door of the cabin. While I waited, the dog patrolled the edge of the property, marking every tree as his.

I tossed him a slice of bologna right from the package and ate four for my lunch, not bothering to put them between slices of bread. Orange juice right from the carton chased down my only meal of the day. I searched the cupboards for cookies, remembering how good Cummings's homemade ginger snaps had tasted. Finding none, I settled for saltine crackers and another slice of bologna with one for Zac, too.

Above the fold of the newspaper, Phoebe American Horse's face stared at me. In her hands, she held a set of elk antlers wrapped in burlap. "Poachers in Park" was printed in block letters.

Maybe those poachers were hunting for me.

I kept a pistol on the top shelf of the closet in the spare bedroom. It was hidden high up, behind extra blankets and pillows. Still tucked in the closet, I kept a few pieces of Jenny's clothes I wouldn't let the girls take from me.

I took the revolver down, thumbed a cartridge into each chamber of Colt Python, and laid the gun on the kitchen table next to Jenny's Bible.

The jangle of the phone startled me. I reached for it.

"Hogan, here."

"Yeah, Hogan, this is Ed Rogers."

"Hey, Ed. What's going on?"

"I'm in a tight spot. Dalton Cummings said you might be able to help me.

"I can try."

"Anyways, Cummings said you might need to get out of town for a day or two. I got four horses that need to be in Grand Lake. You ever pulled a gooseneck with a two-ton?"

"I've done it before."

"And when I said those horses need to be in Grand Lake, I mean they need to be in Grand Lake tonight. If you could get over here in the next hour, we'll get you on the road. I'll pay for your dinner in Grand Lake and you can sleep in one of my wrangler's cabins over there. No hurry in getting the truck back tomorrow. Bring your fly rod along. Heard there's a caddis hatch on the Colorado. You can fish on the other side and come back in sometime late afternoon. It would get me out of that tight spot. Whatya say?"

I eyed the pistol on the table and let out a slow breath. "Let me get a few things together and I'll be right over."

"That's great."

I hung up the phone, changed clothes, and found my sleeping bag. Zac's tail thumped on the floor. He hovered by the front door and tilted his head when I tucked the pistol into my belt.

"C'mon, buddy. We're takin' some horses for a ride."

The dog followed me out the door.

Chapter Twenty-Three

The sun's first rays had barely found Vail's deep valley when Willow guided the Corvette out of the hotel's garage. She bought a large coffee when she stopped to fill the car with gas. Once on the road, she sipped the coffee, reached out to the seat beside her, and patted her uncle's knapsack and its cash.

At the I70 exit, she tucked her hair up under her new black cap and turned east. It was just over one hundred miles to Grand Lake. She'd be there in two hours.

Chapter Twenty-Four

Cadence Tait closed the door to her hotel suite, crossed to the small desk by the windows, and read through the stack of messages the bellhop had brought.

On top was a handwritten note from the hotel manager expressing his sympathy for the loss of her husband and assuring her that the hotel staff would do everything they could to help during these trying times. Cadence smirked at the sentiment, wadded the message up, and dropped it into the wastebasket.

The next several pages were a fax from her husband's secretary in Iowa. Condolences from the governor and other friends, updates regarding arrangements at the mortuary, the first draft of Paxton's obituary for her approval, more notes from those who'd called to express their sympathy. The last page was a neat typewritten page with requests from the media.

She scanned down the list until she spotted the call from a network correspondent in Washington.

She turned sideways and looked at herself in the mirror.

A smile swept across her face. The grieving widow's diet had flattened her stomach.

Cadence left the pages on the desk. The breeze rustled the pine needles on the trees outside her window and dark clouds built along the mountains.

The phone on the desk rang. She answered.

"Ms. Tait, we have a call for you," the hotel operator whispered.

"I asked you people to hold all my calls."

"The caller is very insistent, ma'am. He's called five times in the last half hour." The operator cleared her throat. "He says he's an old friend. He said his name is Tommy. I asked for a last name. He said you'd know who it is."

Tommy? Tommy Bumpus? Her brother had given him strict instructions to never call her. Didn't the idiot know better?

Cadence took a deep breath. "Yes," she said to the operator. "Put him on."

The phone line clicked and a faraway voice sizzled over the static. "That you?"

Cadence felt the warm anger flare along her cheeks. "You were told never to call me. All our communications are to go through—"

"The girl," Tommy Bumpus whispered. "I called about the girl."

Cadance's stomach tightened.

"Go on."

"Usher spotted that red Corvette in Grand Lake."

"Is he sure it's her?"

"He's sure."

"Does my brother know?"

"I tried to call him. Couldn't get through. That's why I called you. He must be busy up in the park. A lot goin' on."

Cadence let out a deep breath. Willow could ruin everything. It was a problem she best handled on her own. "Where can I meet you?"

She scribbled the directions on the back of a page from the bellboy's fax and hung up without saying another word.

Cadence dialed the hotel operator.

"Please, bring my car to the rear entrance. I've decided to take a drive."

Chapter Twenty-Five

I remembered Ed Rogers telling me that for over fifty years his family had been giving tourists horseback rides. If that was true, their barn hadn't been repainted since the first rider saddled up. The structure leaned at an angle that suggested if it would ever topple, the whole building would somersault down the hill and bob down the Fall River through the middle of town.

Smiles beamed from the faces of a family of dismounted riders. They huddled around the Rogers Livery sign and committed their day with the horses to Kodachrome.

I wanted to smile with them, but the image of Hayden Bumpus's thumb snapping forward still filled my thoughts.

I nosed Jenny's car into a place on the up-hill side of the sagging barn. The old building was used for storage now. The stable's office was in a new pre-fab at the back of the property, and saddle horses milled in each of the six pole corrals.

A black Dodge two-ton pickup with a gooseneck horse

trailer had been backed up to the loading chute. Four horses stood side-by-side; halter ropes tied to the top rail. Ed had the left front hoof of a big bay between his knees and a hook knife in his hand. In a motion he had done ten thousand times before, he cleaned the caked mud from the horse's hoof. He saw me, set the animal's foot on the ground, stroked its rump, and came to meet me at the fence.

Ed reached between the top and second rails to shake my hand. "The wrangler I was gonna have do this was struttin' for some tourist girls when he got too close to the back end of an ornery horse. Got kicked halfway into next week. He's gonna be okay, and maybe he learned his lesson." He tapped the handle of his knife on the rail. "Smart money says he didn't."

Ed tipped back a straw Stetson. His eyes narrowed. "Dalton told me all about the poachers. Bumpuses, huh?"

"They arrested Hayden."

He cocked his head and touched his lips with the tip of his tongue. "Ugly scar over his eye?"

I remembered the shiny pink place on the man's forehead, almost hidden by his greasy hair. "Yeah."

"That'd it be, Hayden. Otherwise, those two boys look just about alike. Gettin' you over the mountain until things cool off might be the right thing to do. Hayden can be trouble, but his brother Tommy's the bad one."

"You know them?"

"My wife went to high school with 'em. Hellraisers even then. They live in an old place down the canyon 'tween here and Loveland. Sell firewood, trade junk, and the like. But huntin' and fishin' is what they live for. Just don't think the rules are made for them." Sweat beaded in his thick sideburns. "Year before last, they killed a big ol' buck deer on the front lawn of that church out on Highway Seven. A neighbor heard the shot and saw their truck. People showed up for Sunday morning services and there's a steamin' gut pile on the front lawn. Hayden got arrested for it. Before he comes to trial, the neighbor finds a present on their front porch." He shook his head. "Somebody shot their little girl's German Shepherd, dressed it out like a deer, and hung it from the basketball hoop over their garage door."

My guts knotted. I looked at Jenny's car. Zac's paws balanced on the driver's seatback. The little dog was all I had.

Ed spit between his boots. "Those folks decided a dead deer wasn't worth testifying over. Court had to let Hayden go."

He whistled to two of his wranglers. "Get these horses loaded." He bent and stepped through the rail fence. "You want to spend an extra night in Grand Lake? There's a bunk over there you can use. Don't worry about gettin' the truck back. We can make do without it for a couple of days."

Ed's wife came to the trailer just as the last horse stepped in. Her jeans were as faded as his and her face was just as tan. She looked through the slats in the trailer, made some scribbles on a clipboard, and turned to me. "You're a Godsend, Guy Hogan. It would've been me driving this truck if you couldn't have helped. And I would've had to turn right around and drive back tonight. That's how busy we are this time of year." She perched her hands on her hips. "I don't know what you worked out with Ed, but you'll come to dinner after church next Sunday." She lifted herself onto the toes of her scuffed boots and looked up into my face. "And you'll come this time. I don't know how many times I've asked you and you found a reason not to every time. Guy Hogan, you can't just sit there in that house all by yourself. Jenny wouldn't want that."

If the fear of the Bumpuses knotted my stomach, the woman's words only pulled that knot tighter. "We'll see,"

I told her. "But, thank you." I pressed my eyes to a space between the slats and pretended to look at the horses.

Chapter Twenty-Six

Willow knew that bad men don't get up early. The things that made them bad happened late at night. She'd learned the hard way that bad men sleep late.

It was just nearly one in the afternoon when she made the call from the pay phone in front of Grand Lake's police station.

"Hullo." Last night's beer and cigarettes thickened his voice.

"Usher?" Willow said in the way her mother had taught her. Not like a little girl asking for help and not at all in the I'm-better-than-you dismissal way. She mimicked the tone of her mother's voice when her mother promised something vague.

"Who is this?"

"Willow. We met at my uncle's."

She could hear sleep's confusion melt and imagined him tossing away dirty blankets and struggling to sit up. She wondered if a woman shared his bed. Not that it mattered for her plans.

"Yeah." He coughed to clear the thick phlegm in his throat. "Yeah, I remember you."

His lips were probably pulling a cigarette from a crumbled pack he kept by the bed and she imagined him reaching for one of those brightly colored plastic lighters. If a woman was there, he would be naked. If not, he'd slept in his clothes.

"What's this about?"

She had been planning just what to say since she'd left Vail. "I need to see you." She didn't wait for him to ask why. "Money," she said and added, "lots of money."

He was quiet, then asked, "Will I have to kill somebody?"

It was what she hoped for. It meant two things. First, she had chosen the right man. Next, as soon as they hung up, Usher would call her uncle. "Where can we meet?" was all she said.

—

It wasn't at all what Willow needed.

The Grand Lake police car rolled through a dirt parking lot at the end of the row of tourist shops. Willow pushed down the bill of her cap and adjusted her sunglasses. She shifted on the wobbly wrought-iron chair and peered over the menu in her hands.

The police car stopped behind the Corvette.

Police kept watch for stolen and missing cars. Especially small-town police with nothing else to do. She'd learned, from a rookie cop she dated, that descriptions by make, model, color, and license plate were posted each morning. A red Corvette on the list would have caught the cop's eye. She imagined Barnie Fife double-checking the Texas plate against the number on his call sheet.

She held her breath.

What if the Texans had noticed her scheme and

reported the plates stolen?

But Grand Lake's finest drove away.

She laid the menu on the table and let out her breath. Close. Too close. She'd have to ditch the car. Keeping it was too risky.

A shadow passed across the menu. "Ready to order, ma'am?" The waiter wore tight jeans and a T-shirt with the café's name. He was proud of the stubble on his face and hadn't shaved in two or three days. His hair needed trimmed, and he was staring at her.

"The Monte Cristo." She tapped a finger on the sandwich column of the menu. "Rum and coke," she added and wondered if the waiter was old enough to work in a bar.

"Bar won't open for another half hour."

"Then bring my sandwich and the drink as soon as you can. And when you do, make it a double."

It was nearly four-thirty. The plan was to meet Usher at six. Willow had spent the last three hours wandering the tacky gift shops and predictable art galleries along the main street. She'd strolled the walking path along the lake, watched tourists in rented boats, and smelled the fishy smells on the hands of fishermen. And tried her best not to be bored.

She polished a speck of dried food off a spoon with a paper napkin and considered her new circumstances. She'd leave the Corvette in the parking lot and not dare go near it again. Her fingers touched her purse on the chair beside her. She'd moved the money from her uncle's backpack. That was all that mattered. Her clothes and makeup and anything left in the car couldn't be traced back to her.

The waiter set her sandwich on the table. Fries fell from the plate and left greasy marks on the placemat. She glanced up at him. The waiter winked and set the rum and coke on the table. "My girlfriend's the bartender. She did me a favor. Oh, and it's a double."

She smiled and made sure he saw the smile. "Could I ask you something?"

"Sure." The kid propped the serving tray on his hip and thrust his hips out in a mock Elvis Pressley pose.

She wanted to laugh.

"I thought a friend was going to pick me up. Something's come up. There isn't a taxi in this little town, is there?"

"Yeah. Grand Lake Taxi Company. My girlfriend keeps the number at the bar. Mostly he just drives drunk tourists back to their hotels after closing." The waiter did another crotch thrust. "I'm off at five. Maybe I could give you a lift." He tried a sly smile.

Willow put a hundred-dollar bill on the edge of the table. "Call the taxi. And split the change with your," she paused, "*girlfriend.*"

The kid moved the tray in front of his groin like he needed a shield.

—

Willow nursed a second rum-and-coke—a double—while she waited for the taxi. The waiter gave up trying to charm her.

Usher had told her where to meet him. He hadn't asked her to call back. He picked the time himself. That meant he thought for himself. She could use that to her advantage. She doubted it would take much to persuade the lanky mountain man that what she had to offer was better than his arrangement with her uncle and mother. She had the cash if she needed it.

Willow lifted her drink and rattled the ice at the bartender. When the young woman looked her way, Willow pointed at the glass and mouthed, "One more."

Even the alcohol couldn't chase away the same thought that had haunted her for as long as she could remember.

Make. Her. Hurt.

She would use Usher and the money to get even with her mother for leaving her in a trailer in New Mexico with a father who drank up his paychecks and never wanted a daughter at all. Get even for all the times Willow had called, and no one had answered the phone. Or calls that came only when her mother wanted something.

Make her hurt. Make her doubt. Make her feel alone.

A blurry hand set the third drink on the table.

Willow let out a long breath and plotted her next moves. After Usher's call, her uncle had gotten word to her mother, she had no doubt. Willow would have liked to have been in the magical mirror from some fairy tale to watch her mother cringe at the news her daughter would dare steal from her.

Anger and confusion blended like the spices in the rum.

"Taxi's here." The girl at the bar called.

Willow finished her drink and as she set the glass on the table, she let her tongue lick the last drops from the rim. She pushed up from her chair. Her hand caught the edge of the table to steady herself. A rough spot on the edge of the wrought-iron table caught on the thigh of her jeans and sliced the fabric.

She cursed. Heads around the barroom turned her way. Then Willow picked up her purse and walked to the door.

Fresh air replaced the smell of tourists and burgers from the crowded barroom.

The rum's warmth crowded Willow's brain. Her mother would be pacing her hotel room. Willow could imagine Cadence scratching at her hairline, behind her ears, and at the corners of her eyes. All the places she had paid to have her face lifted and tucked and fixed. All the reminders of the things that she could never make perfect. Like an unplanned daughter—the inconvenience that needed to be hidden and left behind.

—

Her ride was a canvas top jeep. The driver wore a graying ponytail, a plaid flannel shirt rolled up to the elbows, and flower-print shorts. Scaly, hairy calves were jammed into cowboy boots. The gender was ambiguous even when the cigarette-rough voice asked, "Where you headed?"

"Know a place called the Painted Antler?"

"I hang out there sometimes myself. But you be careful," the driver growled, "It can get real rowdy some nights. And whatever you do, don't get suckered into shootin' pool with a fella named Usher."

Willow hugged her purse and her mother's money tight against her lap.

—

Willow plucked a fresh hundred-dollar bill from her purse and handed it over the seat back. "This is good. I can walk from here."

"You sure?" The driver eyed the C-note. "Don't think I've got change for that this early in the day."

"Keep it."

He snatched it from her fingers. "For that tip, I'll drive you to the front door and carry you inside."

The driver meant it to be funny.

Willow didn't care. "Pull over. Now."

The driver swung the jeep into a wide, gravelly spot on the shoulder of the road. A strip of trampled, July-brown grass separated the roadway from the dirt parking lot at the Painted Antler Bar and Grill. A half dozen pickup trucks nosed up to the building like hungry piglets around their mama's nipples. Willow had hustled drinks and waited tables at too many places like this one.

Places where men like Usher spent their time.

Places she'd grown to hate.

The sun was still high in a cloudless sky. In these mountains she had learned dark wouldn't come until close to nine. She didn't so much as wave "goodbye" when the taxi left her at the road's edge.

If she had to make a bet, Usher would be waiting inside. He wouldn't be even a minute late. He had tried to hide the eagerness in his voice, but she could sense it in the sound of his breathing through the phone. Usher—just like the boy at the bar in Grand Lake—would be sorting through the filthy images he had conjured of her. Stalking each filthy fantasy in his mind, like he hunted the elk.

Her mother had taught her about men. *Such fools. So easy to use.*

She tucked the purse under her arm. The faintest breath of a breeze touched her face. The sheen of rum-fueled perspiration cooled her and, with the shiver that followed, goose bumps spread over her skin. She crossed the parking lot, sidestepped between the trucks, and the toe of her boots caught on the uneven ground.

Too much to drink?

She'd have to be careful.

Two men in fishing vests stepped out of the barroom's front door. One, in a battered cowboy hat, smiled and held the door for her. It took a moment for her eyes to adjust from the bright outdoors to the shadows inside. Somewhere in the back, pool balls clicked off each other, and the smell of French fry grease and spilled beer hung in every corner of the room.

From behind, a hand grabbed her arm just above the elbow.

"Look who's here, Ush."

The man was shorter than Willow. He had a dark beard, narrow eyes, and rust-colored stains on his overalls. She knew better than to try to pull away. Instead, she let the short man guide her across the room.

Usher uncoiled from his barstool. He rolled his shoulders, reached behind his back with both hands, and stretched. "Willa, good to see you and you're right on time."

His friend tipped his chin to the barstool next to Usher and nodded for her to take a seat. She lifted herself onto the stool and Shorty pressed a cold bottle of Coors into her hand. Usher nudged his barstool closer to hers and sat down. He rested one arm along the bar and leaned toward her. His free hand touched the top of her thigh and a dirty finger found the torn place in her jeans.

"Drink up, Willa. Your mother's on the way."

Chapter Twenty-Seven

Ed Roger's daughter, Linda, ran their stables in Grand Lake. Light spilled through the screen door of the cabin Linda shared with her husband. The glow of a kerosene lantern lit a half-dozen boys in cowboy hats crowded around a picnic table in the yard. Miller moths swarmed the porch light. Linda stepped out the door as I steered the truck and trailer into the yard. She hooked her thumb and finger in her mouth. A whistle so loud I could hear it over the noise of the truck's engine split the night. The wranglers lifted their heads. All six got up from the table and ambled across the yard to a corral with a loading chute.

Linda tucked a long braid of red hair, the color her mother's must have once been, into the hood of her sweatshirt and wagged a finger for me to back up to the corral.

She met me at the pickup's door. "As soon as we get you unloaded, I gotta call Dad. He's been callin' every half hour askin' if you made it yet. I thought he was gonna order me to send out a posse.”

“Heavy traffic tonight.” Zac climbed into my lap and Linda reached out to rub his ears. “Must’ve been some kind of accident earlier. Wrecker pulled a car out of the ditch just this side of the summit and me and a line of cars followed him pretty near the whole way to town.” I flexed the stiffness out of my hands.

“Flatlander tourist, huh?”

“Most likely. But watch how you say that. Your father says tourist money put you through college.”

She had the same smile as her father. “We’ll take their money, all right.” She winked up at me. “And thank God every day they come to these mountains. Don’t think I could do a real job.”

The trailer gate clanged shut. Her wranglers had the four horses milling in the corral and the trailer unhitched.

“Don’t pay these savages much, but we feed ‘em good. We had a long day, and they started threatenin’ to go work for another stable, so we ate without you.” She slipped her hands into the front pocket of her sweatshirt. “A friend runs a greasy spoon down the road towards Granby. It’s a locals’ place. Mostly construction workers and cowboys. Gets rowdy on Friday nights, but they’ll cook you up a good steak. I called and told him you’d be on your way.” She gathered Zac up into her arms and rubbed her face against the beagle’s. “I’ll feed your pup. You go get somethin’ to eat.”

—

The Painted Antler Bar and Grill sat back from the highway and would have been easy to miss if it weren’t for Linda’s directions and a neon sign shaped like an Indian chief’s war bonnet. The cinder-block building had no windows, just a door not quite at the center.

I parked where the neon haze faded into the darkness,

locked up, and hurried across the lot. I tried to decide if the steak I was anxious to eat would be rare or medium rare.

Fingers of tobacco smoke crawled from the top of the front door and the light's glow turned the smoke into yellow clouds. A too-loud Waylon Jennings's song battered my ears as I stepped into the barroom. Men leaned on a long plywood bar and others lounged at round tables made from cable spools.

The clop of a blonde waitress's cowboy boots on the cement floor somehow kept time with the music. She pointed at me and then jerked her thumb over her shoulder to an empty booth in the corner.

I slipped into the booth. The music paused and the sound of a cue ball making the first break came from a room in the back.

"What ya havin', sugar?" The blonde mashed a red metal Coors tray against her plump breasts and leaned forward.

The lines and creases in her face told me this wasn't her first night on the job. A black hair on the end of her chin sprang up through thick make-up and she'd painted bruise-blue colored half-circles above her eyes. "Kitchen's closing in a few minutes. Unless you want a pickled egg and a bowl of pretzels, you better be makin' up your mind."

"Steak?"

"Rib-eye's tonight's special. Just like every other night."

"Then I'll have the special. Medium rare."

"We'll try for medium. But you'll get whatever comes out." A pink film of bubble gum covered her tongue. She folded the gum back into her mouth and made a snapping sound. "You get fries and green beans with that. Maybe a fresh roll if we haven't run out. Need a beer?"

"Just water."

She shrugged.

Somewhere in the back, a beer bottle shattered on the

cement floor, followed by the roar of men's laughter.

"Local rowdies. Best stay clear of them." She rolled her eyes. "There's a pretty little city girl back there with 'em. All those boys are struttin' their stuff for a chance with her, if you know what I mean." She popped her gum again.

I shook my head. It was none of my business.

"Well, she's lookin' to get herself in trouble. You can bet on that." My waitress looked over her shoulder at the pool room. "A couple of those boys can be bad news."

The laughter quieted. The clack of pool balls striking each other followed.

"Where can I wash up?"

"Men's room's back there." She gave a nod toward the pool room. "And, sugar, you watch yourself."

I skirted the bar and paused at the archway outside the poolroom. A pair of fluorescent tubes hung over the table, making the only light. Round tables, no bigger than hubcaps, lined the walls. Chairs paired each table. There was a butt on nearly every chair.

A short man in stained overalls pointed at the yellow ball with the end of his pool stick and then touched the side pocket. He leaned over the table, sighted on the cue ball, and snapped the stick forward. Cue hit yellow. Yellow spun toward the side hole, glanced off an angled cushion, and rolled to the center of the table, kissing off another ball. Shorty's chin dropped onto his chest.

Hoots and laughter filled the room.

"Damn it," Shorty breathed. He snatched a long neck from the table's edge and tipped the bottom to the ceiling. When he came up for air, he said, "Your shot, Ush."

Smoke haloed a table in the corner. A black cap with *Vail* spelled out in glittery letters shielded a blonde's face. She sat in the lap of a lanky man. Her legs dangled between his spread knees. Red dust clung to a two-day growth of whiskers on his chin. He eyed her like a mountain lion might watch a fawn.

A glass with three fingers of hard liquor, not beer, sat on the table in front of him and a half inch of gray ash at the end of the cigarette in his lips pointed at the floor. His hand moved from the woman's waist, down her hips, and his fingers found a frayed hole in her jeans on the top of her thigh. Two of his fingers explored the hole, and the woman squirmed. Slowly, the cigarette in his mouth stood on end until the glowing red end nearly brushed the man's nose.

The woman pushed his hand away, but he dug deeper. The edges of the denim-hole tore wider.

"Quit playing with her and take your shot, Usher," Shorty barked. He tipped up the beer bottle and his tongue searched the opening for the last drops.

Usher plucked the cigarette from his lips, then pressed the woman's cheek to his mouth. When she fought to pull away, his tongue darted to her ear. He eased her from her place on his lap to an empty chair and stood. The man adjusted the crotch of his jeans and picked up a pool cue from where it leaned against the wall.

I thought the woman would take the chance to move away. But she tilted her face up and looked at me.

It was Willow. The woman from the stream. The one who'd given me a ride in her shiny Corvette. And who I'd seen downtown. Every image from the past days crowded my tired mind.

"This is for you." The words slurred from a tall man's mouth. "We'll win this and get on outta here for some real games." He took a drag from his cigarette and hung the smoking stub on the table's rail.

I moved to the side of the table across from where Usher studied the green felt.

"You're shootin' stripes 'case she made you forget." Shorty dropped his rear end onto a chair at a side table and rested his pool stick between his knees. A full beer had found its way to his fist.

"This 'un." Usher pointed. "Corner." He tapped the table closest to me.

Behind Willow's glassy eyes, some shimmer of recognition stirred.

Usher crouched over the table. He false-stabbed the stick through his fingers.

I spoke. "Willow?"

Usher's face jerked up. He eyed me, and then let the stick clatter onto the table. In two steps he was at her chair. She stood. He grabbed her wrist. She twisted to free herself. His knuckles turned white around her arm.

"This is none of your business, old man. Who do you think you are? Her father?"

Shorty rocked back in his chair. "More like grandfather," he cackled.

Men at the tables pulled their drinks closer. Every eye found me.

I looked at Willow. "Is everything all right?"

"She's with me." Strings of spit hung from Usher's teeth. He wrestled with his grip on her arm. She fought his grasp, struggling to pull away. He forced her arm down. A little girl's noise came from deep inside of her.

Not a cry. A plea.

"Willow, would you like to leave?"

Usher's face boiled red. "I said this is none of your business."

Though everything else raced, I made the words slow and even. I remember what she'd said to me in her car. "Willow, you said you might need a friend someday."

Usher tangled his free hand in Willow's hair and pressed her face against his dirty T-shirt. "She's with me." Alcohol made his voice a feral snarl.

I swallowed away the dryness in my throat. "Willow, do

want to leave?"

Despite his grip on her hair, she twisted her face so she could see me. "Please," the little girl inside her whispered.

For the first time, I spoke to Usher. "She's coming with me."

He tossed her aside like a child's doll. Rage roared from his mouth. He lunged for me.

I snatched his pool cue from the table and swung the butt end for his shins. Wood snapped on bone. His roar turned to pain. Usher toppled to the floor, hands stretching to grab me. I mashed the heel of my boot onto his clawing fingers.

Shorty bolted to his feet, cocking his pool stick behind his shoulder. He swung for my face. I dodged back. His stick cut the air a fraction from the tip of my nose. I rocked forward and slapped the broken end of my cue across his ribs. Air whooshed from his lungs and he slid to the floor.

"Willow, now."

She snatched her handbag from the floor and staggered around the pool table. I wrapped my arm around her waist. Her weight fell against me. Usher rolled on the floor clutching his legs. The short man still gasped for breath.

We backed out of the pool room and into the restaurant. People froze in their seats. I dug in my pocket and jammed a twenty-dollar bill into the bar's tip jar. "For the steak." I nodded to the waitress. "And I'll keep the stick."

Usher stumbled into the room. He caught the end of the bar and struggled to stay on his feet. "She's just a bitch in heat. That's all she is. She'll come back. You watch. She'll be back."

Willow buried her face on my shoulder. I smelled too much beer on her breath. "Thank you," I heard the little girl's voice say.

We backed our way into the parking lot and the night.

"My truck's over there."

Willow tilted her face as if my words had to seep into her brain and replace the alcohol with thought.

"Hurry."

I pulled her by the arm toward the corner of the building. She wobbled up to the pickup, caught the door as I swung it open, doubled over, and emptied her stomach onto the ground. I pushed her inside the truck and tossed the broken pool stick into the darkness.

In the next second, I was behind the steering wheel. I jammed the key into the ignition and we made for the highway. I punched the gas as the front tires touched asphalt and shot gravel from the spinning wheels. The pickup's back end broke around as I turned the wheel. I fought the fishtail to get it back and gunned the truck away from The Painted Antler and Usher.

Willow's head flopped back against the seat's headrest. Vomit clumped in the tips of her hair. In the flat glow of light from the dashboard, the skin I remembered as perfect was ashen and pitted. Smears of tired makeup masked her eyes.

Thoughts wrapped around me as tight as my hands on the steering wheel. *What had I just done? And who was this woman?*

Chapter Twenty-Eight

Cadence Tait guided her sedan down the dark two-lane from the mountainside. She hadn't spoken to Bumpus since the scrawny mountain man had climbed into the car over an hour before. She cracked the window and let the rush of wind wash away the earthy smell that emanated from the man.

The roadway leveled out when they reached the valley floor.

Bumpus stirred in his seat.

"Can we trust Usher?" she asked.

"Only thing Usher likes more than women is money. That's why he called. He knows you've got money. He can always find another woman."

Cadence processed what the little mountain man had said. It meant that she couldn't trust Usher. Or Bumpus. She'd need to be careful.

"Where do we find him?"

Bumpus sat up and pushed his hair from his eyes.

"The Painted Antler. He plays pool there. Bar, just off the highway this side of Granby."

"That means nothing to me."

"We'll pass the turn to Grand Lake in a couple of minutes. Just keep goin'. Five miles more. It'll be on the right. I'll tell ya where to turn."

There was no reason Cadence should have anything to do with men like Usher and Tommy Bumpus. But these men were very good at finding things in these mountains and killing them. After what Willow had done, Cadence needed men who could do just that.

Chapter Twenty-Nine

I checked the rearview mirror for the hundredth time, but no headlights pierced the darkness behind us. Usher and his friend hadn't chosen to follow. I looked again.

They weren't coming.

Not yet.

A wave of dizziness swept over me as the last drops of adrenalin faded from my veins and muscles.

Willow's eyes were shut and was her breath so shallow that a part of me feared she might not take the next. I swung off the highway and followed the road into Grand Lake. On the main street, the clock on the bank building showed nineteen minutes after ten. The day's last vacationers strolled along the boardwalks near the shops, motels, and cafés. Four young men stood at a flickering fire pit in the town's park. Bold letters on a nearby sign reminded that the Park closed at midnight.

My fingers tightened around the steering wheel like the grip I held on the pool stick. A shiver inched down my spine.

What next?

Near the end of Tourist Row, there was a restaurant that stayed open much later than its competitors. Before her sickness came, Jenny and I had eaten there often. Better yet, I remembered the eatery was near Grand Lake's police office.

In case . . .

I decided against parking on the street and headed for the public lot farther down. I eased the pickup into a parking place behind a bloated RV, in case Usher followed.

When I doused the headlights and switched off the engine, Willow's eyes opened. A moan caught in her throat. "Where are we?" She turned and looked out the car's window. Her shoulders trembled.

"Listen, no one followed us. We can go in here. You can clean up. Get something to eat. We'll decide what we should do next."

"No." It was the little girl again.

"It's all right." I pointed. "Look, the police are right there if those men follow us." Two patrol cars sat in front of the office building.

She shook her head. "Why did you help me?"

"You needed help."

Willow twisted in the car seat. "That's not a reason, Hogan. That's your name, isn't it?" She turned to face me and moonlight touched the tear-streaks on her cheeks. "Why, Hogan? Why help me?"

It wasn't Willow I saw. It was the husk that had been Jenny in that instant after life's spirit had left her. When I searched for Willow's answer, the reason was there, but the words were too far away. Seconds became a minute. Jenny's body, as lifeless as the man at the river, filled every place in my mind.

Finally, "Let's just say you remind me of someone." I

croaked out the next words, "Someone I couldn't help." A ball of all my hurt jammed in my throat.

Willow tilted her head. I hoped I would see understanding in her eyes, but the shadows hid her face.

Waves on Grand Lake scooped up the moonlight in silvery spoonfuls. All was quiet.

"It's so pretty here." Her fingers twisted at the tips of her hair. "Look at the town's lights reflecting on the water."

"Come on. Let's go in."

She nodded and mopped her eyes.

I met her at the truck's door. But when I reached out to help her, she pushed my hand away.

—

"We'll take that table in the back," I told the teenage hostess and pointed to a booth against the windows that overlooked the lake.

A starched apron was tied over the girl's fleshy stomach. She plucked two menus from a bin hanging near a cash register and handed them to me. "You can seat yourselves." She yawned.

Willow steadied herself on the counter. One hand dabbed at her eyes.

"*Somebody*'s been partying," our hostess said, just loud enough to be heard.

Willow dropped her handbag on the counter and reached inside. She came up with a wadded bill clenched in her fingers. When she straightened the crumpled money, I saw it was a hundred.

"I'll take one of those T-shirts." She tapped on the glass countertop. This voice came from the woman in the sunglasses, hands on hips, looking down her nose at the Ranger boy, not from the little girl admiring the town's lights on the water.

"What color?" The girl yawned again.

"It. Doesn't. Matter." She said each word as if she were scolding a bad dog. She leaned forward and eyed the girl. "I wear a small."

Our hostess, who hadn't worn a small since grade school, rolled her eyes.

Willow tapped the glass with her fingernails. "Now."

The girl found a black shirt. "This one's a small." She laid it by Willow's purse. "That'll be nineteen-ninety-five. Plus, tax."

"Keep the change." Willow let the hundred dollars fall from her fingers. "Where's the ladies' room?"

The girl snapped up the bill as it touched the counter. "Just around the corner, Miss." The eighty-dollar tip put a smile on her face and courtesy in her voice.

"I'm going to clean up." Willow ran her fingers through her hair as if trying to brush away the cigarette smoke and grit from the poolroom. "Order a cup of coffee for me. I'll be out in a minute." And she was gone.

I wondered who would come back. *The little girl or the woman who gave away hundred-dollar bills?*

I handed the menus back to the hostess. "And bring a cup for me, too. Black." My empty stomach called. "And two cheeseburgers with everything. And a bowl of that homemade chili, if you've got it. Now, where can I find a pay phone?"

"Back there. Near the restrooms." The eighty-dollar smile nodded.

I didn't think Willow would run, but it would be best to stay close. And I had a phone call to make. Digging into my wallet, I found Batterton's business card.

—

Willow let the stall door slam shut behind her. She had the room to herself. She leaned forward, put one hand on each side of the restroom sink, and wouldn't look in the mirror.

She was sober now.

She couldn't lie to herself like she had so many times. It wasn't the altitude. It wasn't that she lost track of time. It wasn't that Usher or his short, little friend had forced her.

It was that one more sip of rum. That one more glass of beer. That one more turned into three more. The one more she'd promised to never do again.

This time it was the Bacardi and coke at the bar in Grand Lake that turned to beer and Bombay Gin with Usher at the Painted Antler.

Don't look. She refused the take just a peek at the mirror. *You know you'll hate what you see.*

She twisted the sink's faucet. Warm water coughed from the spigot. She held her fingers there until it was so hot, she had to pull away. She stripped off the cotton blouse that smelled of barrooms and bad choices, dipped it into the hot water, and scrubbed all the places that Usher had touched her.

"Shit. Shit. Shit." She wanted to scream. *How could I be so stupid?*

She tossed her ruined shirt in the restroom's corner, bent close to the counter, and cleaned her puke from the tips of her hair. Then scrubbed her face with the harsh restroom soap until her skin felt raw and far from clean.

Think.

Her head ached and her stomach rolled.

What now?

Willow struggled into the T-shirt she'd bought. She smoothed the wrinkles from the front of the shirt, enjoying the fresh feel of the new fabric against her almost clean skin. Not daring to look at her face, Willow let herself see the printed words on the T-shirt front in the mirror.

"That fat little bitch," she whispered.

She had taught herself to put on make-up without looking at her face. When you despised what might look back from a mirror in the bus station washroom or the dressing room of a Dallas gentlemen's club, one trained oneself to see only the patch of skin being painted.

Never the whole face.

Lips were the easiest. Lean close to the mirror, purse your mouth, and trace. On her cheeks and forehead, spread the concealer, but do it quick.

Eye makeup was the hardest. But with practice, she had learned never to see who was looking back.

When she had finished, Willow turned to the wall-mounted hand dryer. She pressed the button, bent forward, and fluffed the still-damp tips of her hair in the rush of warm air.

With her hair dried, she double-checked the money in her purse, and then for the first time she looked in the mirror. But just a glance.

Hogan, that's his name isn't it, will expect me to be grateful.

How can I use that?

—

I turned my back to the women's restroom and punched numbers from the ranger's card into the telephone. Behind the door, a toilet flushed, followed by the rush of water into the sink.

Click Batterton picked up before the second ring.

"Click, this is Hogan. Sorry to call you at home." I drew a deep breath. "Especially this late."

"Where are you, damn it?"

"Grand Lake. Ed asked me to haul some horses over here for him. Listen to me."

"No, you listen." Through the phone, the bedsprings squeaked as he struggled to sit up. "There's something you should know. The drowned man you found in Fall River?"

I sucked in a breath. The wet hair, filmy eyes, and cold

touch of cold flesh rushed in. "What about him?"

"His wife—"

My brain saw the woman on the street with Willow. At the hospital to identify her husband's body. The politician's wife from Iowa.

I pressed the phone's receiver tighter to my ear. "What about her?"

"Cadence Tait was supposed to have this press conference up at Park headquarters to talk about her husband and thank law enforcement. Them TV folk that was here for the poachin' story get sent to cover all the doings. Crowd's waiting. American Horse struttin' her stuff and actin' important. But the Tait woman—she don't show. Now nobody can find her." Batterton took a deep breath. "And Hogan, now people are rememberin' things. Like they saw her downtown Estes. With a woman. The same day we pulled the husband outta the river." He paused and let out a breath. "Just like you said."

I glanced at the restroom door.

Batterton went on. "Know somethin' else? That blonde that was there when you found the body? Nobody can find her either." He paused and the stubble on his chin scraped across the phone's receiver. "Hogan, this whole thing's got a bad smell to it."

I curled my lip over my front teeth and bit down. "She's with me."

"Who, Hogan? Who's with you?"

"The girl from the river. Willow Stanford. I'm in a restaurant in Grand Lake right now and she's here with me.

"Jesus Jones, Hogan."

I filled him in about Usher and the fight at the bar.

"I'll make her go to the police," I told him. "Their office is across the street."

"No."

"What?"

His voice changed. "Don't take her to the police."

"Why?"

"This poachin' thing is bigger than any of us thought. Might even be a couple of the deputies from Grand Lake involved."

I tried to take it all in.

Batterton added more. "They're watchin' a state patrol trooper on that side. Think he's got somethin' to do with it, too. Hogan, I'm not sure who we can trust?" His bed creaked. "Sit tight. I'll come get the two of you."

Behind the restroom door, the splash of water in the sink stopped and the electric hand dryer whooshed on.

"No, that'll take too long. I'll bring her to you."

"Hogan?" Batterton's voice came from far away.

The restroom door opened and Willow stepped out.

I hung up the phone.

She patted the damp ends of her hair. "I rinsed it out in the sink." New make-up freshened her face, and a new shade covered her lips. She gathered up her blonde hair and pulled it back into a ponytail. The stenciled image of Long's Peak decorated Willow's new black T-shirt. She glanced down. Above the picture, the artist had added the words *Come Play on My Mountains*. "I think that girl picked this on purpose." When she smiled, she studied my face. "Is something wrong?"

Over the pounding in my chest, I heard myself say, "Yeah."

Chapter Thirty

Bumpus climbed into the passenger side of the car and the man with him opened the back door and slid onto the seat behind Cadence.

Bumpus nodded. "Mrs. Tait this is Ush—"

"I know who it is." She tilted down the rearview mirror and stared at the man. "The girl? What about the girl?"

"You just missed her."

She glared into the mirror.

"She was here with us." Usher looked away. He fumbled with the words. "Pretty drunk. We were shootin' pool and waitin' to hear from you." He looked out the side window. "This old guy comes in. He must have knew her or somethin'. She left with him."

"You let her leave?"

"I tried to stop her, and me and the old guy . . . uh . . . we kinda got in a fight." Usher rubbed his face and looked down.

"Is that why you're limping?"

"Huh?"

"Limping. I saw you were limping when you walked to the car."

"Yeah, the son-ova-bitch broke a pool cue across my shin bones when I wasn't looking and took her." His breath fogged the window.

"Do you know who this man was?"

"Uh-huh, never seen him before."

Cadence shut her eyes and took a deep breath. She hated men like these. "Do you have any idea where he took her?"

"They headed back towards Grand Lake. You must have just missed them."

"Do you have a gun in your truck?"

"Huh?"

"A gun. Do you have a gun?"

"Yeah. Sure. A shotgun and I keep a pistol under the seat."

"Get them. Now." Cadence stepped out of the car and watched the lanky man go to his truck. "Which one of you wants to drive?"

"Where we goin'?" Bumpus asked.

"Just do as I say. And do it now. I won't be inconvenienced."

Chapter Thirty-One

Willow and I took the table at the back of the dining room, where we could watch the lake. Our waitress filled our coffee mugs and set platters loaded with fries and burgers on the table.

A woman had replaced the frightened little girl that had fled the Painted Antler with me. No longer pale and ashen, Willow was beautiful again.

"I didn't realize how hungry I was until I saw all this." She cut a French fry in two and lifted a piece to her mouth with the fork. I picked up a fry with my fingers, searching for the words to ask the question.

"I need to say thank you." She looked out the window. Wind and moonlight swept over the lake's surface, chasing feathery waves across the water. "Men usually cause my trouble, not help me get away from it."

I forced the words out. "Willow, the man we found in the river. He's been identified."

Willow turned to look at me. The coyote greens and

browns of her eyes turned as cool as the water.

"Do you know a man named Paxton Tait?" I lifted my coffee mug to my lips.

Her mouth fell open. "Oh, God. She killed him."

The coffee turned cold in my throat.

"She killed him, didn't she?" Behind her, make-up color drained away.

"She who, Willow?"

"My mother."

It hit me like a gut punch. *The woman I saw at the hospital was Willow's mother?*

"I didn't look at the—the—body," she went on. "It was all too sickening to think anyone was dead like that." Willow turned back to the lake. Cord-like tendons strained in her neck. "She told me we had to be careful."

Her story came too easy. Perhaps too easy to be the truth.

"Is that who I saw you with? Downtown Estes? The evening after we found his body?"

Her eyes squeezed shut. "She told me that night we had to cool things—until after his Senate appointment. For me to go home. And wait." Tears welled in her eyes. "She killed him. I know it. If she didn't do it herself, she paid someone. That's her way. She hates"—she searched for the right word—"inconveniences."

"Willow, you have to tell the police what you know."

"I can't. She'll kill me just like she killed him." She turned to the window. "You don't know how cruel she can be."

Clouds drifted across the moon and the shadows hid her eyes.

"Look, I know a ranger back in Estes. He'll know what to do."

She looked at the restaurant's door like she expected Cadence Tait to step inside.

"No." It was the little girl again, crying out the word.

"You can't let her get away with this. A man was killed." But I was guessing. Maybe the man hadn't been murdered. Batterton hadn't said for sure. His death still could have been an accident.

And Willow had lied before.

"I won't," Willow whispered. "I need to get out of here as soon as I can. I'll go where she can't find me."

"Then I can't help you."

Willow's face turned as flinty as it had when she demanded the waitress get the T-shirt.

It was all I could think of. Just a chance, but I had to try. I sucked in a breath and looked at her. "I'm going to the police. Right now." I tipped my head toward the police station across the street. "I'll tell them everything you just told me." It would mean nothing without Willow to verify it. But I would tell them. I pushed my chair away from the table and stood. Willow turned toward the lake.

I walked away.

Chapter Thirty-Two

Willow watched Hogan's reflection in the window. He would stop at the door. She was sure.

Men always did.

But Hogan never so much as paused. The door swung shut behind him. A cool hint of night air floated across the restaurant and Willow was all alone.

Had it been a mistake to come back for more of her mother's money? Should she have dumped the Corvette in Vail like she had planned and caught a flight out of Colorado? She thought Usher would be easy to play. And then the first rum and coke. How could she be so stupid?

She couldn't be wrong again.

Her mother would be looking for her. Maybe Usher would be with her.

She snatched up her purse and left another hundred-dollar bill on the table to cover their food. Until there was a better option, she had to depend on Hogan. At least for a little while.

She could decide what to do next. There were always options. Her mother had taught her that.

But this Hogan was different from any man she'd known. Others had wanted something of her. Depend on this decent man? Teary-eyed princesses did that in fairy tales.

But, God. What else could she do?

Chapter Thirty-Three

The night's cool mountain air should have refreshed, but it brought no relief. I wasn't going to go to the police. It was a bluff. I'd go back to Linda's stable. Wait there for Batterton. Then tell him what Willow had told me.

And be done with all this.

I stepped from the boardwalk into the street. The truck was in the lot down the street.

A hand tugged at my shirtsleeve. Willow pressed the car keys into my hand. Moonlight painted her face in fresh, new shades, but this time the voice wasn't the little girl's. "Let's find your ranger friend, Hogan. I'll tell him everything." She turned her face and spoke to the dark. "We'll take the Corvette."

—

Like a bubble swept along the ripples of a trout stream, the Corvette glided over the two-lane highway. Outside, pine trees crowded the road's sides. The tips of their branches drew lacy patterns against the slate of the sky.

Inside, silence filled the car. Above the hum of the tires, the rhythm of Willow's breathing rose and fell like she might be asleep, but in the bluish glare from the dashboard, I could see her eyes were wide open.

The gauge on the Corvette hovered five miles over the fifty-mile-an-hour speed limit. Willow pressed the button on the door and powered the window down a few inches. The rush of cool air prickled the skin at the back of my neck. She stuck her hand out of the opening.

"Aren't you going to ask me?" She let the wind dance through her fingers. "What was I doing with a woman who could kill her own husband?"

I tightened my grip on the wheel. "We need to get you to a safe place where you can tell what you know to the law. I don't need to know anything more right now." Though every part of me wondered what troubled this beautiful young woman.

She took a deep breath of the fresh air. "I really don't have an answer. A good one, that is." She leaned back in her seat.

The two lanes narrowed near the log building at the entrance station to the national park. A green light on the dark hut told us there was no need to stop. I touched the accelerator and sped through.

Willow took her hand from the window. She touched the button and the rising glass sealed our bubble, locking the outside world away.

All my life I have solved problems, found the answers, and taken action. As Jenny slipped away, my questions had no answers. Perhaps Willow's didn't either.

In those last days, when Jenny lay dying, there was nothing I could do. No answers to find. When I couldn't save my wife, emotions welled up inside me. Of all that I felt, anger was the only one I could understand. Not a raging anger, but deep inside the seething kind that refused to be quenched. It drove a wedge between me and my daughters that still separated us. That's why there were no phone calls. They feared what might answer.

My refuge in these mountains had turned into a lonely prison. A prison that I couldn't release myself from until Willow pressed the car keys into my hand.

Now I had a task.

I steered the Corvette into the next curve, and we raced from the valley floor up the mountain. Headlights touched the faraway, silvery thread of the Colorado River.

With no lights to signal oncoming cars, I straddled the center line. Past fifty-five, then sixty miles per hour. Like a racehorse begging its rider to free its reins, the Corvette surged at the pressure of my foot.

Weathered guardrails—a blurred notice of the steep drop-off on the right—swept past Willow's window. I tapped the brakes and slowed for the next curve.

Willow's head fell back against the headrest. The glow from the dashboard drew harsh shadows on her face. "Hogan, it's not . . ."

White light blazed in the rearview mirror. Willow whipped around her head to look behind us. I squinted at the glare.

"Hogan, someone's back there."

I reached up and tipped the mirror to keep the brightness out of my eyes. "Don't worry. Just someone like us. Headed over Trail Ridge."

The car behind us was gaining. In seconds, its high beams wrapped around the Corvette.

"God, it's Usher. He's after me." Willow's fingers gripped the headrest. "Get away from him."

The lights behind us disappeared for an instant and then reached out as the car came around the turn.

I studied the mirror. "It's not Usher. There was nothing

but pickups in the parking lot at the bar." I pressed down and turned into the next curve. "That's not a truck following us." The Corvette's tires squealed. "Maybe some tourist in a big hurry." I let up on the gas and steered from the center of the road toward the guard rails. "I'll give him room to get around us." The front tire touched the road's shoulder and gravel pinged off the fenders.

The car behind took no advantage of the clear roadway. It closed to two car lengths. The driver hunched over the wheel and beside him in the passenger seat, the round shape of a man's head leaned close to the windshield. The red dot of a lit cigarette glowed in the passenger's mouth.

My foot jammed the accelerator to the floor.

"It's him," Willow cried out. "Usher found me."

I reached out and pushed Willow back onto the seat. "Hold on." My left hand spun the wheel at the switchback curve ahead. The back end of the car slid around. Sand and gravel from the side of the road sprayed the air. Rear tires found the edge of the pavement, and we rocketed up the incline.

The Corvette's headlights drilled a tunnel of brightness into the dark. The center line slipped under the midpoint of the hood, and the passing guard posts blurred.

Willow braced herself on the dashboard as the car swung around the sharp turn at the top of the switchback.

"Seat belt," I hissed.

She clawed for the harness and strapped it over her shoulder as I fought the car into the next curve. The wispy ends of her hair brushed my face as she swayed in her seat.

Tires skidded. I pressed for more and my mind saw the Corvette missing the turn, crashing through the guardrail, its fiberglass body exploding into a million splinters on the rocks below. My lip curled over my teeth and I bit down, willing the car, Willow, and myself far from the mountain road.

Willow twisted to look behind us. "He's after the money."

I thought of the hundred-dollar bill she bought the T-shirt with. How much more was in her purse?

I checked the side mirror. Only darkness.

"I don't see him," she said.

I eased up on the gas pedal and studied the dark reflection. Like a vapor trail in the night air, a hint of glowing red drifted around the last curve in the roadway behind us.

I mashed down on the pedal. "He's turned off his headlights." I swung the Corvette into the next curve. "He doesn't want us to know how close he is."

Around our hurtling car, there was more sky than trees, as we passed the timberline for the long open stretch of the road across the alpine tundra.

"They're still there," Willow cried. "I see them."

Think. The Vette's advantage is on the curves. Push it. Get away before the road straightens up on top.

We passed the dark buildings at the Alpine Visitor Center. Every bump in the roadway came up through the tires to the steering wheel, jarring my hands and brain.

No. Think. How to lose him?

I checked the mirror. Only black behind us.

How does he see? I checked the mirror. The Corvette's taillights glowed red. *Taillights. He's using our taillights to guide him.*

Like the blades on a rifle's back sight, the two cliffs at the Rock Cut stood guard around the gap on the road ahead.

Maybe I can fool him just enough.

I tapped the brakes. In the red glow of the Corvette's taillights, Usher's car seemed no more than a dozen yards behind.

"Hogan, he's right there," Willow bawled.

I nosed the speeding Corvette closer to the right shoulder.

Make him follow our taillights right into the ditch.

Our front tire slipped from the asphalt onto the gravel. It caught and threatened to pull us into the wall. I guided our car away from the awful rocks, fought to correct, and punched the accelerator. My eyes went to the mirror.

The car's headlights flashed on in an attempt to see where they were. The car jerked to the right as its tires found the soft shoulder, listing toward the solid face of jagged stone. But the sedan righted itself, lurched back onto the blacktop, and, with a rage of its own, dashed after us.

I'd bought a few seconds. Now get away. Get away from him.

The sedan's headlights disappeared beneath the swell and roll of the road. When the lights reappeared, they were farther behind than I expected. Not by much, but the distance between us was greater now.

A haze formed on the inside of the windshield from the cool alpine air. I rubbed it away with my palm and fastened my hand back on the steering wheel.

A thousand stars dotted the night, and the moon bathed the drape of darkness in a silver hue. My heart hammered my ribs, and I forced the Corvette to the center line, pushing the car for every bit of speed I dared.

Trail Ridge Road straddled the treeless apex of the mountain. Across this barren roof of the world, there would be no place to hide. Even if Usher couldn't catch us, he would see our every move. We could only run. I pressed hard on the gas pedal and challenged the car for more.

Altitude's pressure built in my ears, like a slowly expanding balloon, signaling the road was starting down. The speedometer showed eighty-five. In seconds, we would drop onto the long switchbacks on the east side of the pass where that much speed could kill us.

If we were far enough ahead, do I pull over? Douse the lights and hide?

No.

Gotta outrun them. Get to the Ranger Station at the park entrance or to the police in Estes. Safe there.

I touched the brakes at the next curve. The open meadows of the mountain top gave way to the first stunted trees at timberline. The road wound down a shelf carved into the granite and gravel of the mountain. Through Willow's window, a sheer face of cut-rock whipped by. A wrong judgment on my side and the Corvette would tumble five hundred feet or more into darkness.

The roadway widened at the Rainbow Curve pull-off. I searched beyond the reach of the headlights for any car coming our way.

Please, God, don't let there be a car with a family at the next turn.

Sixty-five.

Slow down.

I checked the mirror.

Nothing.

Sixty.

Curve. Slower.

Fifty-five.

Around the curve.

Push for speed. Get away from Usher.

Tighter curve. Gun it.

Too fast.

The steering wheel jerked in my hands. We slid sidewise on the narrow road.

Turn into the skid.

I spun the wheel, trying to correct.

No. No. *NO.*

Our world became a blur of night sky, of mountainside,

guard rail, and the asphalt strip running away from us. Willow's head cracked on my shoulder. My hands couldn't move from the wheel to protect her.

Tires wailed.

Dust filled the dagger of brightness as the headlights cut into the night. My face bounced off the side window glass and the day-old stitches in my cheek tore. Instinct jammed my foot into the brakes and clamped my hands on the steering wheel. The blur of motion jerked to a stop.

Willow.

I wasn't sure if it was a thought or if I'd called her name. "You okay?"

The groan, not words, let me know she was there.

The Corvette had come to a stop just inches from the road's edge. Its engine was quiet. The headlights pointed in the direction from where we'd come. I twisted the ignition key. The engine came back to life. I slammed the gearshift into drive. Metal creaked, but the car refused to move. On the road above us, beams from a car that had to be Usher's touched the cloud of powdery dust that hung in the air around us.

I jammed down on the gas. The back tires spun.

High-centered.

"Get out. Get out now."

I reached across Willow, flung her car door open, freed her seatbelt, and pushed her out of the door. She reached back inside the car and snatched her handbag from the floor.

I jerked up on the handle, threw my shoulder against the door, and the latch let go. I scrambled to the other side of the car, grabbed Willow's hand, and pulled her close.

Her body tightened and her eyes showed the fear from deep inside her.

I tugged her to the road's edge. Lodgepole pines stabbed up through the darkness. Below, the steep, rock-strewn slope disappeared into the black.

Was it ten feet from the trees? Or twenty?

The lights from Usher's car pierced the dirty air.

"Jump." I pulled her after me.

Chapter Thirty-Four

Cadence braced her hands on the seatback in front of her as Usher forced the car out of the switchback. A cloud of grit swallowed the headlight beams, and the tires jolted over something in the roadway. Through the dirty haze, she spotted a jagged rock bigger than a basketball in front of the car. Usher swerved to miss it. Smaller rocks battered the car's underside, jarring the floorboards.

A string of foul words spilled from Bumpus's mouth and dirt from outside swept up through the vents and coated the inside of Cadence's mouth and nostrils.

Then there it was.

The red Corvette sat on the edge of the roadway. Its headlights pointed at their oncoming car, as if its driver had poised for some medieval joust, and at any second the Corvette would rocket up the hill.

"Damn it." Usher jammed the brakes to the floor.

Both doors of Willow's car hung open. As the cloud of dust around it settled, Cadence spotted the ruined rear quarter panel and bits of red fiberglass strewn like pieces from a child's puzzle along the twisted guardrail.

Bumpus was out of his door before the car stopped. He jerked a pistol from his belt and sprinted to the Corvette.

Usher slid the car to a stop, inches from the Corvette's front bumper. The lanky man jerked a twelve-gauge pump from the seat beside him and racked a shell into the chamber as he met Bumpus at the Corvette.

Bumpus bent to look into the open door. He straightened, looked back at Cadence, and shook his head. Usher turned from the car and swept the forest above the road with the muzzle of his shotgun.

Cadence propped the car's door open with her knees. "Find them."

Chapter Thirty-Five

Half running, half falling, we slid down the slope. I pitched forward onto the gravel. A sharp stone sliced through my jeans and took a chunk of flesh from just below my kneecap. I bit my tongue to hold in the scream that wanted out.

In the night shadows, Willow shifted her purse to the other shoulder, hooked her fingers under my arm, and helped me stand. I tested the leg. Pain shot to the pit of my stomach, but bone and tendons held. Willow pulled me forward, and we slid-stepped-fell into the forest. The gravelly soil became pine needles under my feet.

In a dozen more strides, Willow pulled me down behind a boulder nestled in a stand of shoulder-high evergreens. The smell of pine trees mingled with the scent of our fear. A cool stone under my knee brought a few seconds of relief from the throbbing.

Above us, at the edge of the roadway, the gleam of two sets of headlights backlit three silhouettes.

"…flashlight…" One of their words drifted down the hill to our hiding place.

I waited for the beam of their light to search the trees, but none came.

"…damn it…" The same voice.

"Here, take this," the other man spoke. "It's loaded."

Guns. They have guns.

"Bumpus, you know where we are?" It was a woman's voice.

I strained to hear the answer.

"Think so. It's real steep. They'll have trouble gettin' away from us in the dark."

First, the headlights from Usher's car went dark, then the Corvette's. As moonlight replaced the harsh glare, my eyes separated the trees from the shadows.

Willow edged closer until her breath touched my face. Her head rested on her purse and her blonde hair shined almost white in the gray moonlight.

I touched a finger to my lips, dug into the dirt beside me, took a handful, and smeared it into her tangled hair. When I finished, I rubbed two fingers of the black soil across her forehead and mixed it with the tears on her cheeks.

Feet crunched gravel on the roadway above us.

Willow dug at the base of the nearest tree, and more gently than I had touched her, painted a mask of dirt on my forehead, and bloody cheek. With a last touch of her fingers, she turned my face to hers. "I'm sorry," not even a whisper.

Above us. "Watch it…" It was the woman's voice again.

Stones tumbled down from the road's edge.

Boots slipped on the gravelly slope. "Aw shit—"

Quick steps on the gravel stopped on the carpet of pine needles, perhaps twenty long steps from where we hid. A hint of tobacco floated on the wind. The red dot of a cigarette dropped to the ground. A foot mashed out the spark.

"See anything?"

"They couldn't have gone too far." It had to be Usher's voice.

Willow pressed tight against me. Neither of us dared breathe.

"Spread out. Work your way down the hill." It was the woman. "Don't hurt the girl."

"What about the old man?"

"I said, don't hurt the girl."

Bile rushed from my stomach and burned my throat.

Hands snapped off branches and feet shuffled over the forest floor. Usher stopped in a moonlit gap in the trees and studied the tangle of branches in front of him.

I twisted my face against the rough rocks so I could see his shadowy form through the trees. I couldn't be sure where the others were, and I didn't dare move to check.

Usher fumbled inside his jacket, lifted something to his lips, and tilted his head back. Moonlight glistened off the bottle in his hand.

"I told you no more of that," the woman barked. "I need you to be sure of what you're seeing."

Usher took another drink and rubbed the back of his hand across his mouth. He cocked his arm and tossed the bottle. In a second, the sound of breaking glass scattered through the forest. Then all went still.

The other man moved down the hill two steps. The woman waited on the roadway.

"Listen." It was Usher.

Above the pounding of my heart, I strained to hear more.

"Truck comin'."

The groan of a straining engine and sounds from shifting gears drifted up from below.

"Damn it," the woman cursed. "Usher, get back up

here."

"What about them?" the other slurred.

"You stay where you are and watch for the girl."

Usher scrambled up the hillside. As the coming headlights rounded a curve, he lifted himself onto the roadway near the woman.

Her words carried down the hill. "I'll do the talking. When whoever's in that truck will see the cars. They'll want to call the police. We don't need that." She stepped back from the edge of the road.

In the next moment, I heard a second engine and another set of headlights lit the road behind the slow-moving truck.

Batterton? He was coming. He'd promised me. But it was too steep to climb up to the road to warn the driver. Any movement and we'd be an easy target.

I lifted my head as much as I dared. A boxy panel-van lumbered around the curve and the silhouette of a pickup followed close behind. Both pulled to a stop near Usher's car and the ruined Corvette.

"What happened here?" asked the van's driver.

The dome light in the pickup flickered on and a man in a dark cowboy hat got out. "Yeah, what happened?"

I knew the voice and hope warmed me.

Betterton was here. He'd see the Corvette and put two and two together.

The woman stayed at the edge of the shadows. "Not sure. Looks like there were rocks in the road. Maybe they hit the guardrail and lost control. We've looked but can't find anyone."

"There's an emergency phone at Rainbow Curve. I'll stop and call the Rangers," the van driver said. "Tell 'em you need help."

"No need. A car came through just before you did." The woman lied. "They said they'd stop and call."

"Whatcha gonna do?" the driver asked.

"We can push it onto the shoulder." The voice I recognized spoke. He'd come from Estes as he promised. "We'll turn on its flashers so no one gets surprised coming around the corner," Batterton said. "That's all we can do for now."

I was sure now. *Sure, it was him. But didn't he recognize Willow's car?*

"Need help?" It was the van driver again.

"No," Batterton called out.

Was Batterton pretending? Was he afraid the van's driver could get hurt?

Batterton's shadow moved closer to the boxy van. "Best thing is for you to get goin' before someone else tries to get through here," he said. *Was he giving the man a message?*

"Okay." The driver hesitated, then, "I've got deliveries for the visitor center up on top. Sure you don't want me to call?"

"No," the woman answered. "The other driver promised he would."

My insides turned watery and my knee throbbed. I had to let Batterton know where we were. Willow supped in a gasp. I raised my head for a better look.

A sound, sharper than thunder, cracked the night. A bullet smashed the tree limbs above my head and splinters showered our hiding place.

"Damn it," Usher bellowed.

"I saw him," Bumpus called up the hill.

The driver in the van shouted, "Hey, what's going on—"

Batterton's hand moved from his hip to the truck's window. The muzzle flash from his gun lit the night.

Everything that I thought I knew turned to ice.

Chapter Thirty-Six

Willow's tears cut pathways through the dirt Hogan had smeared on her face. She folded her arms under her chin and peered up the hill. The voice came again.

The woman's voice.

She knew it. Like she knew the beats of her own heart and the breath in her lungs. It was her mother's voice.

And the man in the cowboy hat?

Her uncle.

Her mother and uncle. Both of them. They were hunting her on this mountain.

Chapter Thirty-Seven

With the back of his hand, Batterton wiped the blood splatters from his face. Smoke from the pistol shot hung in the air. He turned away from the dead driver.

"Did you have to do that?" Cadence hissed.

Batterton stepped close enough to see all the places on her face where the surgeons had done their work. But nothing had changed the woman he knew. "So, your brother is going to clean up your mess again, Cadence. Or whatever you call yourself. It's just one more dead man."

He jammed his pistol into its holster and shouted down the hill. "Bumpus, you fool. You couldn't wait until this guy drove off, could you?" The old ranger tipped his head to Usher. "You and Bumpus push the Corvette off the edge, then push the van after it. Make it look like an accident."

Bumpus climbed up to the road. Batterton grabbed his arm. "You sure you saw them?"

"Just the man."

"You hit him?"

"Don't think so."

Batterton peered into the darkness below. "Shove those cars over the edge," he said to Usher and Bumpus. "We got people to kill."

Chapter Thirty-Eight

Willow tugged at my arm. "We have to go now. Before they come after us."

I pried my fingers from the rocks, looked at the darkness below, and then turned to look back at where Batterton had murdered the man. Numbness filled me. I needed to wake up from this terrible dream.

Willow pulled my arm again. "Now, Hogan." She tugged me to my feet.

With each step, the forest closed in around us. I dodged face-high pine boughs. Brush clawed at my feet. Only the pain that stabbed at the raw wound on my knee let me know that this dream was real.

We zig-zagged down the hill. The gleam of the headlights on the road melted away. Treetops caught the moonlight before it could find its way to the ground around us. Like an enemy plotting with Usher, Batterton, and Cadence Tait, darkness wrapped tight around us.

We moved a step at a time. Touch the rough bark of

a pine tree. Reach out with a foot and probe for the next place to step. The hillside dropped steeper. I clung to the trees to keep from falling. Willow clung to me.

My foot slipped off a slick stone and pain shot up to my battered knee. "I need to rest." I breathed the words at Willow's shape just inches from me.

"No. Keep going."

With her next step, Willow's ankle gave way. She fell against me. Her feet shot out from under her and she sat hard on the rough ground.

I hurried to her. "It's too dangerous. It'll be light in a few hours. We'll wait. It's all we can do."

I felt her nod. In the gloom of the forest, a tinge of her perfume drifted on the chilled air.

"How far have we come?" she asked between breaths.

"A mile. Maybe more."

"Do you know where we are?"

I tried to pull in all the places I had hiked, the streams I'd fished in, and the maps I studied. "If I'm right, it's another three, maybe four miles to the bottom. There's a road and a campground in the valley. We can find someone to help us. It's steep and rocky all the way down, and it'll be hard."

I peered up through the trees for some small clue that my guess was right. Currents of icy wind touched my face. This north slope would be the last to see the sun in the morning and the coldest place on the mountain tonight. "All we can do is wait."

Willow's fingertips tangled in my shirt. She moved closer. I pressed my back onto a tree and held her.

A rumble came from the road far above us. Trees groaned and snapped. Rocks toppled down the hill.

"The truck," I whispered. "They've pushed it over the side."

A picture of the lifeless body stuffed into the vehicle painted itself on the back of my eyelids. The image had

Jenny's face.

More crashing sounds came down the hill.

"Your Corvette. They're making it look like two cars went over."

Her hand grazed the wound on my knee. "How bad is it?"

"Just tore the skin. I'll be okay." Pain throbbed with each pulse of blood, and I prayed it wouldn't stiffen and keep me from running when I needed to.

Willow's teeth chattered. "I'm so cold."

I twisted to pull off my jacket.

"No," she said and wriggled against me. "Just let me hold you. We'll keep each other warm."

The chill from her skin sliced through her thin T-shirt, onto my flesh, and into my bones. I wrapped my arms around her shoulders and pulled her close to me.

She rocked back and forth. Her face rested on my chest and she held me like my girls had when their nightmares came.

Above us, the very tips of the pine trees clawed at the sky like black skeletons. Only the sounds of our breathing filled the space around us.

As the dark settled over us, I tried to make myself believe that the man I thought was my friend had just killed the driver of the truck.

Chapter Thirty-Nine

"Hurry." Cadence gritted her teeth and tapped her foot on the pavement.

Batterton stepped to the driver's side of the Corvette, reached in through the open window, and turned the steering wheel. Usher and Bumpus moved to the back of the red car.

"Now," the ranger said.

Usher and Bumpus heaved up on the back bumper. The car rolled from the pavement onto the gravel. Batterton braced his shoulder on the window frame and the three strained. The front tires hung for an instant on the very edge. Dirt and soil crumbled away and then, in a single motion, the car rocked forward like a child's teeter-totter. The weight of the engine completed the fulcrum, and the car disappeared into the dark drop-off. Sounds of snapping trees and twisting metal rose from below.

"Don't let them get away," Cadence ordered.

"They can't have gone far." Batterton shook his head.

"Too steep and dark down there. If we push, they'll just run. We need 'em wonderin' what we're up to. They'll get scared and find a place to hide. That's what we want." He walked to his pickup. The ranger opened a toolbox bolted to the back of his truck's cab. He took out a foot-long black flashlight and flicked it on.

"Got something besides that shotgun?" he asked Usher.

"My poachin' gun." He tapped his belt. "Twenty-two pistol. Don't make much noise. Use it for head shots." He licked his lips.

"Let Bumpus have the shotgun and you use your pistol."

Cadence paced the road's edge. "Whatever we're going to do, we need to hurry."

Batterton pivoted to face his sister. The beam of the flashlight twisted shadows across her brother's face.

She stepped back. Batterton's teeth glistened in the dark.

"Killin' that man made me the boss for what we have to do now." He pulled his jacket away from his hip. Moonlight played over the pistol he had just used. He looked at the three. "You'll listen to me until we get the girl and the . . ."

Cadence waved a hand. "I don't care about him. Just her. Alive." She nodded to Bumpus and Usher. "Okay. We'll do what you want, won't we?"

The two poachers mumbled their yeses.

Batterton pointed with his chin. "Flashlights and a lantern in my truck. Up around the next curve, there's an old maintenance road left over from the ski area. We'll hide our cars there. Bumpus, give Cadence your pistol. She's used one before." He turned back to his truck and pulled a scoped rifle from behind the seat.

As Cadence took the handgun, she looked into Bumpus's face and tilted his head ever so slightly at her brother. "Keep a close eye on him," she whispered to the poacher. "And remember who pays you."

Chapter Forty

Willow stirred in my cramped arms. "They'll come for us, won't they?" she whispered.

I nodded into the pitch-black around us.

She answered with a shiver.

"Willow, what do you have that she wants?"

She didn't raise her face. "She's the one killing the elk."

I knew Bumpus was involved. But Cadence Tait? "Are you sure?"

"I'm sure."

"What about Batterton? Is he part of it, too?"

Her head moved against my chest. "He's my uncle. He works for my mother."

The words hit like a gut punch. Thoughts spun in my head. Batterton couldn't be involved. *But he's killed the driver.*

I struggled to pull the pieces together.

According to Batterton, elk antlers brought big dollars in the Far East. Dalton Cummings, the game warden, said what was happening here in the national park was something bigger than Hayden and Tommy Bumpus could pull off on their own.

But Cadence Tait? The woman who had just lost her husband. A husband who was about to be appointed to the United States Senate. And now Batterton?

It was too much to take in.

"Why?" I whispered.

"It's always the money. Are you that naïve?"

She moved to look up at me, but night shadows hid her face. "She has people killing elk in Jackson Hole and in Montana and up in Idaho. It's bigger than you can imagine."

Willow pulled away. "Not everybody in this world is as good as you are." She shivered in the cold. "She used her husband for the money. He said no more. That's why he's dead."

I wanted to see her eyes when she spoke, but the night forbade it. "What's in your purse?"

"Just like in a bad movie, it's all written down in a little black book. I took it. I have the names. Who paid who? Which banks have the money?"

"Batterton? His name's there, too? And, you're sure?"

"You really don't understand, do you?"

Her words bit into my core like the cold around us. If what she said was true, it explained so much.

If it was true.

I'd caught her in so many lies before. She'd lied then. Why not now?

I lifted my wrist to check my watch. By the faint glow of the fluorescent spots on the watch face, it was a few minutes after three. By five, it would be light enough to see. I had two hours to sit tight and wonder how much of what Willow had said was true.

—

With a twitch, my chin jerked off my chest, and I opened my eyes. Darkness still shrouded the forest.

"You fell asleep," Willow whispered.

"How long?"

"Not long."

"I shouldn't do that. We need to keep watch."

"I would've woken you if I'd heard anything." She rested her head on my chest and the little girl spoke. "Maybe they're not coming."

I said the word even though I knew it was a lie. "Maybe."

"No. She never gives up."

The ground turned colder. My knee throbbed as I moved to find a bit of comfort.

Willow huddled closer. "What time is it?"

I lifted a cold-stiff arm and looked at my watch. "Another hour 'til sunup. Can you hang on 'til then?"

"I think so."

She rubbed her icy hand down my wrist and over my fingers. She paused at the wedding band I still wore.

"You're married," she whispered.

"My wife died ten months ago. Cancer."

"You loved her, didn't you?"

"Very much." I wondered if anyone had ever loved Willow like I loved Jenny.

—

I searched the sky for any hint of the coming sun and bit back the shivers. Far up the hill, in a black knot of trees, a speck became a small white dot. From the spot, a shaft of light flowed out until it faded, overpowered by the night. The beam swung to the right and then arced back to the left, sweeping and spying where it could.

Slowly, the cold-fueled dullness in my mind sharpened.

Flashlight. Batterton. Willow's mother, Usher and Bumpus. Hunting us.

Like they hunt the elk.

"Willow." I caught her face in my hand and turned it toward the light. "There."

She struggled to stand.

I held her down. "Wait. We need to see what they're going to do."

The beam from the flashlight disappeared and then stabbed out again.

"Stay still," I whispered to Willow.

I rolled up onto my hip, slipped the folding knife from its sheath on my belt, and opened the blade.

An old adage played through my mind.

Never bring a knife to a gunfight.

But what if a knife is all you have?

Chapter Forty-One

Cadence Tait struggled to keep her feet on the steep, rocky slope. "Where do you want me?" She tangled her fingers in the branches of a stunted bush to keep her balance.

"Just stay close." Batterton lifted his chin to Bumpus. "You move out there maybe fifty yards."

The round-faced little man nodded and left the group.

"I'll take Cadence and we'll follow Bumpus." Batterton wiped his mouth with the back of his hand. "Usher, remember how you told me about how you and the Bumpuses hunted up that big bull elk?"

Usher's eyes flashed in the darkness. "Sure do." He nodded.

"You hang back and see if you can make it work again."

Batterton handed a flashlight as long as his forearm to his sister. "When you get out there aways,"—he pointed with the gun barrel"—turn on that flashlight."

"They'll see it," Cadence hissed.

"That's what I'm counting on."

Chapter Forty-Two

I couldn't remember how long it had been since yesterday.

Finding the man's body in Fall River was years ago, and the promise of dawn seemed just as far away. A sliver of moon, the color of a worn silver dollar, touched the far mountaintops, but no light found its way to the shadowy place where we hid.

Willow crowded close beside me on the carpet of pine needles. When her fingers wrapped around the wrist of the hand that held the knife, all the warmth in her seemed gone. From far above us, the sound of breaking branches filtered down the hillside. On the slope above, the yellowish beam of the flashlight probed the trees.

Looking for us.

"How far?" Willow whispered.

"Half a mile." It was a guess.

"We need to get away."

"Listen." Through the crisp morning air, the snap of breaking branches cut the stillness. "If we run, they'll hear us like we can hear them."

"We can't just stay here." Her nails dug into my wrist.

"Yes, we can." I moved my face closer to hers. "It's all we can do."

I checked the light. It veered up the valley, away from our fragile sanctuary. "If we stay still, they might pass by us in the dark."

"Then what? Climb back up this mountain? It's too steep." Fear pushed a shiver through her.

"Hush." I pulled my arm from her grip, found the back of her head, and stroked her tangled hair. "We'll just wait for their next move." I forced calmness into my whisper. "We have to wait."

Jenny would have prayed. Her faith was strong that way. In all the hard times that life brought, she would pray first and then make the decision. Even when the disease ravaged her, she held faith.

I forced a prayer but kept one eye on the light on the mountain.

Treetops above us creaked in the night air. Another branch cracked. The light disappeared into the forest. When it appeared again, it was moving farther away.

"Stay still, Willow."

High up, where the ridgeline met the sky, the black faded and a band of gray took its place. Minutes stretched. A red crescent edged over the mountain top. Across the valley, spear points of golden light chased away the shadows on the slope. Day had found the mountain top but like a coffin, the lid of night refused to open.

Then, the flashlight's beam moved toward us. Twigs crunched under their feet. Here and there, a muffled word stirred the still air. I imagined the pistol Batterton had killed the driver with still in his hand. Without so much as a word, Willow and I matched our breathing to our hunters' movements. Breathe in with their sounds. Hold when they were quiet.

Their light swung away from us. It traveled across the hill and down.

"They're passed us," Willow hissed.

"Shh—quiet." I raised my head as the light moved away.

The new day's light touched the pine needles at the very tips of the branches above our heads. In the dimness, I could make out the contours of the hillside for the first time. To our left, the hill sloped down and away from where we hid.

Suddenly, the silent forest came alive in a flurry of breaking branches. The ghostly shapes of two deer bounded stiff-legged away from the men on the hill.

Now's our chance. Their noise would hide ours.

"Now."

Willow was on her feet. Handbag clutched tight to her side, she scrambled over the fallen trees and disappeared into the shadows. I checked for the flashlight. The beam still moved away from us. Awkwardly, I lifted myself from the ground and limped after Willow.

Sunlight found its way to the valley below us. I could make out where the paved road made a lazy *S*-curve across Horseshoe Park. At a low bridge, the road crossed Fall River, divided the valley in half, and followed the river downstream toward Estes Park, only a dozen miles away.

Upstream, a pale plume of smoke from a fire in the Endo Valley Campground, lifted in the morning air. Tents and cars were specks in the shadows, but they promised people. People who could send word to the Rangers. People who could give us water and food. People who could help us.

At the bottom of the shallow ravine, she paused. But Willow's back was to the valley and the hope it offered. She watched the terrible hillside we had descended in the dark. Her arms crossed over her chest, pressing the purse tight to her breasts. As a shadow passed over her face, her lips trembled.

Usher stepped out from the dimness of the forest. Filtered by the trees, a ray of light glinted off of the silvery pistol he held waist-high. "You fell for the hunter's trick. Old Click Batterton guessed right."

He trained the handgun at my stomach. "Send the beaters out to make noise and wait for the game to slip out the back," he said. "Now, drop the knife."

I clenched my fingers tight around my only weapon. Usher and Willow stood twenty steps away.

"The knife." He jabbed at me with the muzzle of his handgun.

My muscles tensed to spring, but I knew his bullet would stop me before I could close the distance.

"Now," he barked.

I let the knife fall from my hand.

Willow was at his side before the knife touched the ground. "He has the money." She pointed at me and reached for his free arm. "He knows about the money from the antlers. My uncle. Your friends. Everything."

A thousand icy spiders' feet galloped down my spine and my stomach went sick.

"How does he know?" Usher raised the gun higher.

"He works for the Feds." She said it so easily. "He tricked me at first. He told me he knew you. That he was one of your poachers. But I know now. He told me."

Usher glanced from me to Willow. He snaked his arm around her waist and brought her closer to his side. "What happened to the notebook? Your mother wants that book."

I searched Willow's eyes, but the greens and browns grew cold.

"I told you—he took it from me." Her fingers found his free hand, and she pressed his palm over her breast.

Anger replaced confusion, and I hated her.

A smile spread over Usher's face and his thumb released the pistol's safety. The firing pin clicked into place over a live cartridge.

Air refused to fill my lungs.

He motioned with the gun barrel. "Where is it?"

In a blur, Willow caught hold of his gun hand with both of hers. "Run, Hogan," she screamed.

She pushed the gun out and away from his body. He twisted to free his hand, but Willow held tight. Her face snapped forward, and she sank her teeth into his wrist. He wailed out in pain.

Help her.

I lunged for them.

Usher grabbed Willow's hair with his free hand and pushed her head away. Blood smeared his forearm. Willow refused to give up her grip on the hand with the pistol. They wrestled for control. The pistol disappeared between their bodies.

A sound shattered the quiet and the shockwave from a gunshot slapped my face. Usher staggered backward. The gun fell from the space between them.

I smashed my shoulder into Usher's chest and we tumbled onto the forest floor. I dug a finger into the corner of his mouth. His fingers gouged at my eyes. When I pulled away, he wrenched loose from my hold and dove toward the gun. Through the blur of my tears, I saw Willow kick the gun across the ground.

Usher's foot glanced off the side of my face. I clawed a fist-sized stone from the ground, but before I could use it, he was on his feet and disappeared into the trees.

I fumbled in the dirt for the gun, found it, and pointed at where he'd been.

"Willow?"

I checked again for Usher. The sounds from his footsteps moved up the hill.

"Willow? Are you—"

I turned back to the woman who'd saved me. She sat on the ground, her back resting on a pine tree. She'd pulled her knees up close to her, like a little girl playing jacks, and looked down at something in her hand.

I crawled across the ground to her. Blood filled her cupped hand. Just above the point of her hip, a shiny spot wet her black T-shirt.

"Oh God, Willow."

She raised her face. Pasty, pale skin showed where the tear streaks had washed away the dirt on her cheeks. Her lips moved, but no words came.

"Willow, he shot—"

"It hurts." And her next breath rattled up from deep inside.

As gently as I could, I lifted the hem of her T-shirt away from her stomach. She flinched at my touch. Blood seeped from an angry, puckered hole in the softness of her belly. Her breath came in short, shallow gasps.

Shock. She's going into shock.

"Willow, I'll help you."

But what would I do?

I checked the hillside for Usher. *He could be close, waiting to strike. Or had he gone to find Batterton, Bumpus, and Willow's mother?*

No. Help her. Help Willow.

All the first-aid courses I'd taken played like a movie in my head.

Keep her warm.

I pulled off my coat and hung it over her shoulders.

Make her comfortable.

"Willow, can you lie down?"

"No," she whimpered. "It hurts."

"Okay, stay still."

The bleeding. That should have been first. Stop the

bleeding.

I lifted her shirt again. Blood oozed from the ugly puncture. I let my fingers run over her back, searching for where the bullet had torn through her. There was no hole, but when I touched her hip, I cringed when I felt the shattered bones beneath her skin.

God, no. The bullet was somewhere inside her.

Once, during hunting season, a friend had shot a deer in the paunch. With no blood trail to follow, we searched for the animal until it was too dark to see. The next morning, we found the buck bloated and stiff. The ground around it was torn from its last hours of agony.

Willow was bleeding to death inside.

I pressed my eyes shut. *There's nothing I can do. She'll die.*

Like Jenny.

Willow winced with a cough. She touched her lips with her fingers.

God, don't let her lips be red. Don't let the bullet be in her lungs.

No blood foamed at the corners of her mouth.

Thank you.

I fought to breathe. To figure out what to do next. Willow needed more than what I could do for her.

Dirt and filth from our night on the mountain streaked my shirt. I stripped it off and wriggled out of my undershirt. I wadded the T-shirt into a pad and pressed it onto the wound on her stomach. "Hold this against you."

She lifted her face. Her eyes were thick and glassy and the coyote colors refused to blink.

Do I carry her? My battered knee would barely hold me. The hill was too steep. Batterton and Usher were out there somewhere. Batteron had to have heard the shot.

"I need to go get help."

"Nooo," she moaned.

"Willow, I have to." A lump filled my throat, and I saw Jenny on the white sheets of the hospice bed.

"I'm going to go to the campground in the valley." I plucked a stray pine needle from her hair. "I'll call for the Rangers and have them bring a helicopter. Everything's going to be all right. I promise."

"Hogan, stay with—"

"Take the gun." I laid it on the ground and placed her fingers over it. "In case they come back."

I closed my jacket around her, grabbed my dirty shirt, and struggled to my feet. In the valley, the sun sparkled off the side of an aluminum trailer. Fall River shone like a silver ribbon.

"Hogan." Her hands touched her purse. "Her book. You have to take it."

I lifted the strap from her shoulder and opened the handbag. Beneath a tangle of wadded tissues, next to a hairbrush and make-up, the black notebook nested between bundles of hundred-dollar bills still in the bank wrappers.

More cash than I could imagine.

God, Willow, what is this all about?

I took the notebook from her handbag and tucked it into the waistband of my pants.

"I'll be back for you," I said one of Jenny's prayers that I'd make it back in time. And that I'd understand what was truth and what was a lie.

Her head drooped forward until her chin touched her chest. Each breath became an effort.

I scooped my knife from the ground. It was two miles of fallen trees and deadfalls to the campground. Maybe more. Out there somewhere, Usher, Bumpus, and Batterton were waiting for me.

Chapter Forty-Three

A tumbled maze of lodgepole pines, slick with green moss, covered the hillside. Branches reached from the shadows and grabbed me like some curse that refused to let me go farther. Night's chill hung in the stillness and dust danced in the angled beams of light. I struggled over a waist-high tangle of logs. The sun's warmth stayed just beyond my fingertips. It teased and dared me to battle the steep slope.

If her mother found her, what would she do to Willow?

Usher and Bumpus were out there somewhere. Perhaps the silenced rifle they'd used to kill the elk was aimed at my back.

The man I thought was my friend was with them. Would he use the same gun on me that he used to kill the van's driver?

And why, Batterton? Was it as simple as Willow's answer? "It's always the money. Are you that naïve?"

I looked back to where I'd left Willow. It had taken a

half-hour to come maybe three hundred yards down the steep hillside and over the cross-hatch of fallen trees. Sweat streamed into my eyes. With each labored effort to lift myself over the next barrier, my legs grew heavier. Cool air stabbed the raw wound on my knee.

Except for the snatch of sleep, while we waited for dawn, there'd been no real rest in more than a day. Nothing to eat since that bite of food in Grand Lake. Six? Seven hours ago? Nothing to drink in that long.

Willow had to be thirsty, too. Her lifeblood was leaking away a drop at a time. Maybe it was best to climb back. Not let her be there alone.

I stayed with Jenny to the end. Held her hand until the last breath left her.

Still, the nightmares blamed me for not doing more.

Willow shouldn't be alone.

No. Get help. Don't let her die.

I swung my leg up to the top of a fallen log, pulled myself up, and balanced there.

Then I heard it.

Like the sound of wind in the very tops of the trees. I checked the sky. Nothing but the day's new blue and high white clouds. On the slope across the valley, sunlight sparkled off the little creek that threaded down from the far ridgeline through the pines to the green meadows below.

The sound grew. Like the hum of a far-away jet coming closer.

A chipmunk skittered across the ground between my feet. A squirrel chattered in a nearby tree. In the valley, birds of every size left bush and tree and, in a great swarm, took to the sky.

Then the mountain roared.

Across the valley, a brown wave of water taller than a house spilled down the mountainside. Trees snapped like toothpicks in a giant's hand. Boulders, bigger than cars, bounced like rubber balls. The churning mass spilled off the mountain, carrying trees and rocks with it.

In less than a minute, the wall of water churned the valley floor like a witch's cauldron. Bushes, then treetops disappeared beneath the flood. A white-capped wave swept across the muddy stew of torn limbs and up-rooted trees, slapping the forest at the bottom of the hill from where I watched.

Mist from the surge touched my face.

Where? Where did it come from?

The tiny figures of people from the campground up the valley emerged from their tents and trailers. Hands pointed. Arms gathered their loved ones close.

The torrent reached the paved road that divided the valley. Logs and debris jammed under the bridge. The water paused, then spilled onto the asphalt. It trickled over the roadway and into the meadows on the other side.

I thought the road would stop the surge, but the pavement buckled from the weight of the torrent and spilled down the hill. Estes Park, my friends, and Jenny's house would be next.

They had to be warned.

But Willow.

An eerie silence replaced the whoosh of water. I turned back to where Willow waited for me.

I promised I'd be back with help.

Fresh, raw earth showed in an angry slash on the far hillside, but no more water spilled down the mountain. Waves rocked the surface of the muddy lake that seconds before had been a green meadow. The white trunks of uprooted aspen trees bobbed in the flood.

Then I spotted Willow's mother. Just ahead of the water, Cadence Tait ran along the crumbling road.

Chapter Forty-Four

It was quiet and loud all at the same time.

Not a sound from the forest. No squirrel chattered. No birds called. Even the wind dared not stir the trees.

But the noise from the water was everywhere.

Water splashed on the slope below me. It slammed the debris that dammed the bridge over Fall River. Water sloshed over the cement footings and spilled across the cracked pavement and into the meadows. Chunks of asphalt heaved up and slid away. In a great gurgle, the roadway beneath it crumbled.

Just steps ahead of the pooling water, Cadence Tait sprinted down the edge of the roadway. A green Park Service truck jammed on its brakes. Its driver threw the truck into reverse and backed toward Cadence. She pulled open the passenger door and jumped into the truck. As the sludge of floodwater oozed onto the terrace of meadows below the bridge, the truck sped towards Estes Park.

She was safe, and her daughter was dying on the

mountain.

There was no way for me to cross the flood. The campground where I could find help was cut off by the waters.

The weight of the water on the debris under the bridge won its battle. Concrete burst from the pressure and snapping steel railings wailed like a woman's shriek. Water poured through the breach. Not the irate torrent that charged from the mountaintop. This flood was slow and determined.

The flowing sludge sought every low part of the valley below the bridge. The mire filled the river channel, slowed, and the mix of mud, tree branches, and stones oozed downhill. Cadence and the driver of the truck would have time to warn the people in Estes Park.

I had to save Willow.

Faraway, brakes squeal. Coming from the west, a car headed for Estes Park skidded to a stop on the roadway above the stew of mud and trees that had burst the bridge. It paused for several long seconds. Then its driver twisted a U-turn and hurtled back up the hill up Deer Mountain toward Trail Ridge Road.

At the top of the hill was a junction. A right turn would lead over the mountains and back to Grand Lake. Turn left, and the road led to the main entrance and Park Headquarters. There would be help there. It was the long way, but my only choice.

I screamed Willow's name. I wanted her to know I wouldn't give up.

Chapter Forty-Five

Cadence Tait grabbed the door handle with both hands. She wrenched open the truck's door. "What's happened?" she screamed at the driver.

Cadence looked back from where she had just come. The black road asphalt heaved upward, then crumbled away. The trunk of an aspen tree as big around as her waist bobbed in the murky water against the bridge she had just run across. In the next instant, a coming surge of water slapped the concrete and steel of the bridge. The aspen snapped like a matchstick and a wave of dark water spilled through.

"What's happening?" she screamed again.

"I don't know." Fear trembled in the man's voice. "Get in." The driver pulled her into his truck. "I've never seen anything like it. Something broke loose up above," the driver bellowed.

He gunned the engine, and the truck hurtled down the highway toward Estes Park. Half the roadway fell away.

The driver swung his truck to the far shoulder as the terrible stew of brown water swallowed up the earth.

"Shitfire. We gotta do somethin'." The driver picked a path on the shoulder away from the disintegrating asphalt. "There's people in the campground down below. We gotta let 'em know about this."

"No." Cadence grabbed the man's arm and turned him to face her. "Do you know who I am?".

"Those people, ma'am." He pushed her back into the seat.

Cadence took a breath. Tears filled her eyes. Not from fear, from anger. Bumpus and Usher were still on the mountainside somewhere. They'd find their way out. Her brother would be safe. It wasn't her daughter that concerned her.

It was the money. And what was written in the book.

—

I found a narrow game trail that quartered the hillside. The path threaded through the dark trees and underbrush. I'd follow it as far as I dared, then bushwhack across the hillside for the road and the cars that I hoped were still there.

Dampness hung in the air so thick around me that it threatened to steal my breath.

Push harder.

I shoved branches out of my way, stumbled over the wrinkled tree roots, and climbed over rocks. My battered knee throbbed and threatened to fail.

With each stumbling step down the hill, trees and brush crowded tighter around me. Pine needles jabbed the raw places on my skin and branches clawed at my shirt. I lost sight of the road. The thick veil of trees hid any sight of the floodwaters. But I could hear the slosh and gurgle as the flood moved down the hill.

God, let Cadence Tait and the man in that truck warn the people in town, and then let me kill her.

In some great gesture of power, the flood had washed every odor from the air. The smell of the pine trees was gone. The musky, damp scent of the shady places had fled. Not the slightest hint of the wildflowers floated in the air. When I lifted a hand to wipe my face, even the smell of my sweat was missing. I smelled fear and nothing else.

My knee buckled. I caught hold of a pine tree to hold myself up. A cloud of gnats swarmed my face. Though I wanted to lift my hands to whisk them away, I had no strength. The tiny bugs settled on my sweaty skin.

She'll die if you give up.

Another step. The knee held. One more. Sticky blood caked along my shin, stretched and pulled with the next step.

But I took one more. Then another and another after that.

I touched the place I tucked Willow's notebook into my belt.

Aspens took the place of the pines. I was closer to the valley floor. I grabbed a tree in front of me, pulled myself to it, and reached for the next.

Keep going.

Chapter Forty-Six

Each painful breath was a raw dare to take the next. Willow no longer felt pain but saw it as vivid colors. First red. The red smeared and dripped away like her blood. As the red faded gray took its place. Gray seeped from the air. It stole every other color until each shade grew darker.

Black was coming.

Willow heard the voices. When she tried to turn her head, her muscles refused and her head lolled onto her shoulder as if Willow was that favorite Raggedy Ann Doll in the trailer she shared with her mother in New Mexico.

"Over there. See. Like I told you. On the ground." *Was it Usher?*

Had he come back for her?

"She still alive?"

Fingers touched her throat. "She's cold and look how blue she is around her lips." He made a choking sound. "What'll we do?"

"Get the purse. Missus Tait'll want the purse."

Willow's fingers could not hold on to the strap. The bag slipped away from her hand and off her shoulder. Her body slumped over.

"Damn," the man choked.

The gray's blurred darker. "Look at this. A whole shit-load of money in here."

From far away, a loud rushing noise whispered above the forest.

Then, "What was that?"

"Let's get out of here," the other shouted.

Willow needed to speak. Ask for their help. If she could smile, the men would see how beautiful she was. They wouldn't leave her.

Speaking and hearing twisted into one. But words wouldn't come.

She willed the thought to the men. Look at me. I'm beautiful. Help me.

The closest man reached out with the toe of his boot and touched her.

Then the black came.

Only black.

Chapter Forty-Seven

Three cars clustered in the middle of the road as if their confused drivers had no other choice. The cars' occupants stood close by. No one spoke. All stared at the muck that moved down the hill like a slow ogre and the mass of water that took away the bridge.

"Help me," I croaked.

The tallest man in the group turned his head.

Again. "Help me."

His eyes focused on me. He raised his hand. "Emma, look."

I stumbled the last steps from the forest to the road. The man and a woman stood back, not willing to come closer.

"Is that blood?" The woman caught hold of her husband's arm.

Willow's stained my shirt and mine soaked the leg of my pants.

"Are you hurt?"

"Yes, but—" I stepped towards them. "Willow needs help."

"Willows?" The woman tilted her head, not sure of who or what I was.

"I left Willow. She's hurt bad. She needs help."

"Was it the flood?"

"She's dying."

The man reached out. The others only watched.

I was screaming. "Please. We're wasting time. Give me your car."

"Carl." The woman grabbed the man's arm and stepped behind him.

"Emma, he needs us."

Chapter Forty-Eight

My helpers turned their Cadillac into the lot at Park Headquarters. Cars jammed every available parking space. Scores of people gathered at the front doors. Others hurried to the building from the cars they'd left along the roadway. The air buzzed with the sound of people talking and the same questions were everywhere.

"Where did the water come from?"

"What do I do now?"

"Are we safe?"

I pushed my way through the crowd. A woman saw my blood-soaked shirt and stepped back. Children pointed at me. Their already-confused parents pulled their kids closer. I caught hold of the railing at the short set of stairs leading to the front door of Park Headquarters. A knife-sharp pain sliced through my head, and my stomach whirled.

The door to the visitor center opened and a Ranger I didn't recognize stepped out. The noise from the anxious crowd increased. The Ranger shoved her way through the swarm of people, climbed onto a bench, and raised her hands.

"People," she said.

The crowd moved closer, blocking the stairs so I couldn't reach the doors to the office building.

"People, I'm Ranger Maggie Tipton. I've been asked to explain what we know so far."

Maggie Tipton took a deep breath. The flat brim of her park service hat shaded the top half of her face. She exhaled, paused a second, and began.

"Shortly after dawn this morning"—she glanced down at a half-sheet of paper in one hand—"a highly unusual volume of water flooded Roaring River in Upper Horseshoe Park. We believe —"

"Believe?" someone shouted and people grumbled in their confusion.

Maggie raised her voice. "We believe one of the earthen dams somewhere on that upper drainage failed. Until we can get one of our people in to take a look, that's all we know." She eyed the crowd and continued. "Upper Horseshoe Park is flooded. The flood waters are following Fall River downhill toward Estes Park. Because of the topography in the area, the water has spread out and is moving slowly. Evacuations have been ordered."

The Ranger checked her notes. "A team has been sent to check the safety of campers at Endovalley."

Slowly, I made sense of what she was saying. Those were the campers I had seen. Where I was headed to find help. They were safe. Trapped but safe. I wanted to shout it out, but the pain in my head stopped me. I gritted my teeth, turned, and elbowed past the people on the steps.

Over my shoulder, Ranger Maggie continued, "We know that the bridge over Fall River has been compromised and Lower Horseshoe has also been flooded."

I'd seen the water tear the road away. And Cadence

Tait get across just before it broke apart.

"Aspenglenn campground, just downstream, has been evacuated." She jammed the paper in the back pocket of her uniform pants. "Before I came out with the report, we were told that the Cascade Dam at the old hydroelectric plant on Fall River has failed. We're expecting a three-to-six-foot wall of water in downtown Estes Park sometime in the next hour."

I edged closer to the visitor's center front doors.

"What should we do?" It was a woman's voice in the crowd asking what everyone wondered.

I didn't wait for the Ranger to answer. I pushed my way into the offices.

A half-dozen Rangers stood at the counter that typically welcomed visitors to the park. I could see they were studying a map. Their conversation was hushed.

A man with his back to me glanced at the hallway of closed doors. "I wish she'd tell us what to do," he said. "There's got to be a place where we can do some good. Waiting for her to decide is killing me."

Heads around the map nodded.

The floor under my feet turned rubbery. I reached for the wall to steady myself. "Help." The word barely formed in my mouth.

The Rangers were around me in seconds. They took me to a chair.

"Mr. Hogan, it's me, sir. Phil Taylor."

I recognized Ranger-boy's face. His fingers pulled back the front of my bloody shirt.

"You hurt, Mister. Hogan?" And to the Rangers, "Get him some water."

Feet shuffled around me but I kept my eyes fixed on Taylor.

"What happened, Mister Hogan?" Taylor said.

A coffee mug of water was in front of my face. I gulped

it down.

"Get him some more." Someone pulled the empty cup from my hand. "Tell me what's going on. Were you in a car accident?"

"No." But images of the chase on Trail Ridge flashed in my mind. I felt Willow's Corvette slam into the guardrail. *Willow.* "Willow was shot."

"Huh?"

The mug was back. "Drink this."

I drained the cup in a single swallow. My stomach cramped and pain stabbed my chest. My eyes shut and I fought the blackness. *Tell him where she is.* I drew in a breath. One of Jenny's prayers formed in my mind, and I pleaded for strength.

Then words came in spurts. "Willow. The girl who was with me at the river. Dead man."

"I remember." Taylor nodded.

"Shot in the stomach."

"Someone shot her?"

The next cup of water was pressed into my hand. "Drink this slow." He held the cup to my lips and pushed my hands away when I tried to take it from him.

Moisture filtered into the fibers of my muscles and found its way into my brain. Dizziness stayed away.

"On Trail Ridge." I was a bit stronger. "Cars off the road."

"Is he talking about the truck and sports car we got the report on?" someone asked from the back.

I nodded. "Chased us"—pain pounded my brain— "down from Trail Ridge."

"Who, Mr. Hogan? Who chased you?" Taylor pleaded.

"She's dying." I looked back at the young ranger and the others. Their faces began to blur. "You haftto go now." The pain threatened to split my head. "Please."

"Someone get search and rescue on the phone," Taylor

said.

"Every one of them is downtown Estes," a voice answered.

Taylor looked down at the floor and rubbed his face. "I don't know . . ."

The door to the back offices swung open.

Phoebe American Horse was two steps in front of four frantic-faced rangers. "Has anyone heard from Batterton?" she shouted.

Her words stabbed my heart.

"Batterton," I croaked and tried to pull away from Taylor.

My tongue stuck to the roof of my mouth. Everything about the flood, Willow, Cadence Tait, and Batterton, stuck there with it. Taylor's hand held me down. Icy trembles shot through my hands. When I twisted in the chair, Willow's notebook stabbed my stomach. I tried to stand.

"Hogan?"

My eyelids went heavy.

Something like sleep reached out and grabbed me.

Chapter Forty-Nine

illow's fingers touched my shoulder.
Black turned to shades of brown.

The brown of the curtains was just darker than the walls. Tan metal bars just inches from my face matched the blanket draped over my chest.

Hospital? They took me to the hospital?

I tugged my arm out from under the blanket. From a white strip of tape on the back of my hand, a plastic tube led to a pouch of liquid hanging from a silver pole.

When I lifted my head from the pillow, the base of my skull filled with pain and the room swirled into beige and white clouds. I caught hold of the edge of the bed. Metal rattled, and the noise stabbed my ears.

Willow?

"Mr. Hogan?"

My eyes went shut.

Again. "Mr. Hogan, can you wake up?"

Fingers touched my shoulder. The voice became firm.

"Mr. Hogan, we need you to wake up."

I forced my eyelids to open.

The woman standing next to my bed wore a red sweatshirt. *As red as the blood that filled Willow's hand.* My body jerked at the thought.

"Easy, Mr. Hogan. You're in the Estes Park Hospital. Do you remember being brought here?"

I clamped my eyes shut. Images collected behind my eyelids. Someone shouting Batterton's name. American Horse was there. Park Headquarters. Water. Flood.

Willow?

Help Willow.

I opened my eyes and struggled to sit up.

The woman pushed my shoulders down. "The doctor gave you something to help you rest. You might be dizzy. I want you to lie still."

My lips peeled away from my sticky teeth and I croaked out a name. "Willow."

"Is that the woman you told the Rangers about?"

I summoned strength. "Have they found her?"

"Not that we've heard."

"I-I've got to—"

"You have to rest." It was an order. "There's too much going on right now, what with this flood and all for me to have any trouble from you." Her fingertips found their way to my wrist. "We've been blessed. No serious injuries to speak of. But who knows what will come through the doors next?"

She dropped my arm and pulled the thermometer from my lips. "Everything looks quite good."

"But Willow?"

"I told you, no news yet."

"But—"

"Rest, Mr. Hogan." She lifted the plastic tube, took a syringe from the folds of her dress, and slipped the silver needle into the plastic tubing.

"I need to know—"

Warmth filled my hand, flowed into my arm, and sleep's waves rushed over me.

"I'll be back to check on you later, Mr. Hogan."

Chapter Fifty

Sunlight reflected from the shiny enamel on the walls.

"Nurse," I croaked out, then louder, "Nurse."

The woman in the red sweatshirt came to the door.

I lifted my head from the pillow. "Willow—did they find her?"

The nurse shook her head. She came closer and took the thermometer from a glass on the bedside table.

"Answer me."

"There's been no word from the Park Service." She moved the thermometer towards my mouth.

I shook my head and pain rattled around my skull like loose gravel. "What time is it?"

"Nearly three."

Cobwebs untangled from around my brain and I tried to sort out the hours. *Dawn—maybe five-thirty this morning. I left Willow just after dawn. I promised I'd be back. Now three. Nine? Nine and a half hours. Willow had been on that mountain for nine and a half hours. Alone.*

With a bullet in her stomach.

My head dropped onto the pillow. I turned my face from the nurse.

No chance.

Willow was dead.

The nurse spoke. "I'm sure they're doing everything they can to find your friend. What with the flood and all, it's been difficult getting information." Then, as if she read my mind. "Don't give up."

She dropped the thermometer into the glass on the table with a clink that jarred my brain. "I can give you something to help you rest."

"No."

"It might be best."

"I said no. Tell me about the flood."

The nurse moved closer. "They think Lawn Lake Dam gave way early this morning."

I remembered the wall of water spilling down the mountainside. The spray touching my face. Trees and rocks tumbling into the valley.

The nurse went on. "The water followed Fall River right into downtown Estes. I've heard the mud is as high as the doorknobs all along Elkhorn. It swept across the highway and into Lake Estes. But the dam held there. Otherwise, it could have been as bad as the Big Thompson flood a few years back. God blessed us, but it's a mess downtown."

She lifted my arm and searched for my pulse.

I thought of the people in the campground and the tourists' cars that lined the roads. "Was anyone hurt?"

"We've had sprained ankles and cuts and bruises through here all day. A shop owner from downtown came in with chest pains. Poor man had his whole life savings tied up in that store and now it's a muddy mess." She laid my arm back by my side. "I just heard on the radio that there are two dead. Seems these people went back to Aspenglenn Campground to get their things and got caught in the flood. They'd been warned not to go back, but went anyway. Drowned trying to save a pop-up camper and some sleeping bags." She shook her head.

"You said they went back?"

"Yes, the reports we've heard said that after the wall of water got from Lawn Lake to the valley floor, it spread out and filled the meadows up. Then, like a bathtub, it overflowed and surged towards Estes. They'd evacuated the campground and all of downtown. That's what makes those two deaths so foolish. Those people went back, and they were told not to."

I remembered waves of water filling the river channel and then spilling over the banks at Horseshoe Park. Knee-high stalks of grass waved in the current and then disappeared as the water grew deeper. Places where I'd fished covered with water deeper than I was tall.

"You know something else?" she asked. "Remember that politician's wife? Her husband had drowned in the park earlier this week?"

My guts clenched. "Cadence Tait?"

"Yes. Cadence Tait." The woman nodded. "She's something of a hero. She was in the park hiking. She wanted to be by herself to think, she said. The flood hit. A park worker found her and the two of them got the word out that the flood was coming. Without them, things could have been a lot worse." She made some notes on a clipboard hung from the end of my bed. "Now get some rest, Mr. Hogan. The doctor will be in to see you soon."

—

"I'd like you to stay the night." The doctor tucked a pen behind his ear. "You were dehydrated when they brought you in. Dangerously so. And extremely agitated. That's why I ordered the sedative." He took a penlight from the pocket of his white coat, flicked it on, and moved it back and forth as he watched my eyes. "We re-stitched that cut on your face and put a dozen more in your knee. X-rays show no broken bones. We'll get you scheduled for an MRI as soon as things settle down." He tucked the light back into his coat. "You'll be sore for a few days. I'll prescribe something for the pain. I want you to stay off your feet as much as you can and get plenty of rest."

"Then let me go home. I'll rest there."

"Mr. Hogan, you've been through a lot. I want to be sure it was the exhaustion that caused you to lose consciousness, not anything more serious." He took the pen from behind his ear. "I'm waiting for some test results. If everything looks good, we'll let you go in the morning." He scribbled some notes on my chart.

"I want to go now."

Chapter Fifty-One

Tired lines wrinkled Ardell Roger's forehead. I knew neither she nor Ed had had any rest since the flood, but when I called for a ride home from the hospital, Ardell had come.

She wrapped a plastic bag of crushed ice in a towel and handed it to me. "That doctor said to keep an ice pack on that knee. You're going to do what he said, Guy Hogan. You're lucky it's not broken." She watched to be sure. I pressed the cold pack onto my leg. "Just sit there and rest. I'll send someone over with your supper, and I want you still in that chair when they get here. You hear me?"

"You don't need to send—"

"I do, too. And I will." She spread a blanket over my legs. "I talked to my daughter in Grand Lake this morning. Your little dog is doing just fine. We'll find a way to get him back to you when all this settles down."

"The doctor said I should feel better by tomorrow."

"This isn't tomorrow. And that's not what he said. He

said you needed to rest." Her hands found their way to her hips, and she stared down at me. "I need to get back and help with the cleanup. We intend to be renting horses tomorrow if we can. I sent Ed to help the others that weren't as lucky as we were. Some folks lost everything they had."

She switched on my television. "Sit there and watch this."

As the door shut behind her, I took the ice from my knee and dropped the bag onto the floor. Her truck's engine started, she slipped the vehicle into gear and pulled away. I struggled to my feet, limped across the room, and plucked Willow's notebook from the plastic bag filled with my dirty clothes.

The grainy shapes of a news show from Denver played across the TV screen. Tractors pushed waves of mud down Estes Park's main street. Shopkeepers armed with snow shovels pushed watery ooze out the front doors of their businesses. Everyone wore hip boots and mud streaked each face.

The television reporter said, "Damages are estimated to reach twenty million dollars. A third body was recovered this morning."

Did they find Willow?

"The body of a man thought to be the backcountry hiker with permits to camp at Lawn Lake was discovered this morning near the Roaring River."

I shook my head. I could have been that man. Off alone, enjoying the backcountry and swept away by a flood no one expected. I hoped that man had died quickly, not suffered like Willow.

She had to be dead now. Didn't she?

I bit down on my lower lip until it hurt and settled onto a chair at the kitchen table. With the image of her body lying on the mountain haunting my mind, I opened the black notebook and scanned the first few pages.

Willow had said that besides the elk kills in Rocky Mountain National Park, the poachers were at work in Glacier, Yellowstone, and the Grand Tetons.

Willow said this was bigger than I thought.

I snatched my reading glasses from a coffee mug filled with pens and pencils next to Jenny's Bible. I started through the black notebook.

Past the pages with the kill tallies from the other National Parks, I found a single sheet with four sixteen-digit numbers. I stared at each for a second and then grabbed my checkbook from the corner of the table. Comparing the strings of numbers in the notebook with the account number on the bottom of each check left me, no doubt.

From the dollar totals listed in the notebook, I decided nearly two hundred thousand dollars had been deposited into those bank accounts.

Tattered edges of paper clung to the spiral spring where pages had been torn from the notebook. Other pages showed scribbles I couldn't decipher. Just inside the back cover, folded into quarters, I found a neat piece of paper as thin and translucent as onion skin. Carefully, I unfolded it. Faded colors showed it was the receipt copy of a post office money order.

I adjusted the glasses and squinted at the faint writing. The money order was for seven hundred and fifty dollars made out to Tommy Bumpus. But in bold handwriting, the issuer's name was plain. Batterton had signed as the sender.

I had prayed for a bit of evidence. Here it was. As fragile as the thin paper.

Across the room, Cadence Tait's face flickered on the TV screen in a rehashing of praise for the false hero. The screen flashed back to the newsroom, and the reporter broke in. "We've just received this from the National Park

Service. A fourth victim of the Estes Park flood. A woman's body was found in Horseshoe Park. Identity unknown."

The fourth had to be Willow.

Forever etched in the fibers of my soul, Jenny's face would shine as clearly as on our wedding day. But Willow, this woman I had known only those short, few hours, had already begun to blur. I remembered her hair, but not the exact shade of blonde. Even the coyote colors of her eyes began to fade. But I remembered the blended smells of my sweat and her perfume as we huddled together on the cold mountainside. And the thick taste of her blood in the air when I'd left her.

I looked away from the television.

Something as evil as Cadence Tait hatched inside of me.

In a kitchen drawer, I found the set of U.S. Survey maps Jenny had given me. I rolled out the maps on the kitchen table and slid Jenny's Bible onto the paper's edge to hold the top map flat. I found the place on Trail Ridge Road where I believed I had lost control of Willow's Corvette.

I traced where Lawn Lake had spilled into the Roaring River and flooded the valley. Across the green-shaded meadowlands, with my fingertip, I tapped the terraced ground on the opposite hill where Willow and I had hidden through the night.

With my eyes pressed shut, I thought back on those minutes on the mountain. The air grew colder. Pine scents teased my nose and fear wrapped around me again.

Batterton's voice drifted on the breeze. "Bumpus, you know where we are?"

How did Bumpus answer?

"I think so. Hayden and me cached some of the antlers down below. It's steep. They'll have trouble gettin' away from us in the dark."

I stared down at the twisting lines and green shades of

the map. *Where had the brothers hidden the antlers?* If I could find it, there might be something there that could help trap Cadence Tait and her brother.

It seemed like so much to search, to find that one spot. Then my finger rested on the markings for the Lawn Lake Trailhead. I'd parked there the morning I'd climbed the hill to look for evidence of who had shot at me and walked right into the middle of the Ranger's trap for the poachers. Hayden Bumpus had been arrested. I was certain that Tommy had got away that morning.

If I was right, Tommy would have crossed Fall River and climbed the hillside. Did it make sense that he would have gone to where they hid the antlers? A place he knew? A place they would have picked because it was hidden from prying eyes?

Contour lines on the map's hillside made a deep V. The lines were spaced farther apart than the lines on the steep slope where I'd left Willow. An unnamed stream followed the V to Fall River. Maybe I wanted it to be there. I wanted to make more sense of it than I should.

Chapter Fifty-Two

Outside, the sun was setting. Shadows filled the corners of the room. I stared down at the map on the table for the tenth or twentieth—maybe hundredth time. I wanted to see something different, but no matter how I tried, my eyes always went to the stream. I was sure now. As sure as I could be. It had to be the way Tommy Bumpus had slipped away from the Rangers that morning.

A girl wrangler from Ardell's stables had brought Jenny's car when she brought my supper. She also brought orders from Ardell that even though the car was here, I was to call if there was anything I needed and not to drive until the doctor said it was all right.

I stood up, telling myself that my knee was better and that by morning I'd be able to drive. When I took a step, the pain stopped the air in my lungs.

Outside, gravel crunched in the driveway and headlights lit my front windows. Dalton Cummings climbed out of his Department of Wildlife pickup. He choked a brown paper bag around the neck of a bottle and took the steps to my front door two at a time. Flecks of mica sparkled in the gray mud that streaked his pants.

The door swung open. Without so much as a glance my way, Cummings crossed to the kitchen and found two water glasses in a cabinet over the sink. A pint of Old Yellowstone whiskey appeared from the bag. He unscrewed the lid and splashed two fingers into one of the glasses. Cummings held the bottle up for me.

I shook my head and eased into my chair. I didn't dare mix the pain medication with the whiskey. I'd need a clear head for what I planned.

"No, you're gonna need this." He added a half inch to the bottom of the second glass and brought it to me. "You heard they found a woman's body?"

"It's her, isn't it?"

He shrugged his shoulders. "Nobody's talkin', Hogan. They're all scared of that American Horse woman. It's like she ordered this flood to show everyone how important she is. When she's not parading in front the TV cameras, she makin' a hero out of that Tait woman." His eyes peeked over the rim of his glass. "Know something else? No one's heard shit from Batterton. It's like he disappeared."

Cummings gulped down the rest of his whiskey and reached for the bottle. "I heard what you told the rangers . . . 'bout him killing the truck driver.

"Anyways that Taylor kid got the makings to be somethin'. He's the one that found the body. Followed your directions down that hill from where they found the Corvette and the truck."

He took another sip.

I looked away. *It wasn't her. Willow was still alive when I left. Nowhere near the flood and she was alive. Barely alive, but alive.*

Cummings's voice went quiet. "Taylor told me that he

went to where he thought you had told him you had left the woman. That's where he came up on this spot of ground. Said it was near covered with blood. In that bloody mess, he found a crisp new hundred-dollar bill. It was blood-soaked." He leaned closer. "Make sense to you?"

A place in my mind watched a crisp hundred-dollar bill drop from Willow's fingers onto the counter of the restaurant in Grand Lake. And the bundles of new money tucked beside Cadence Tait's black book in Willow's purse.

I nodded.

"That wasn't where he found the body. He'd searched all around. He'd given up and was on his way out of there when he found it. Down the hill in the flood water." He looked at the bottle like he wanted more. He drew in a deep breath. "The body had been in the water for who knows how long. All the clothes were tore off, and it'd been tumbled around by the flood somethin' awful."

My mind recoiled at the image his words painted.

Cummings shook his head and continued, "I got somebody I know at the sheriff's department to tell me this. When the sheriff ran the California driver's license, she showed Taylor where you found the man's body. It came up as a phony. And the Corvette was rented at the Denver Airport with another bad license and a stolen credit card. The kid workin' the desk must have been too busy tryin' to look down the front of her shirt to notice anything wrong. Now get this. She signed the rental agreement 'Wilma F. Stone.'" He nodded at me and then slowly said, "Wilma Flint Stone. Awful cool. Makes me think this wasn't her first rodeo."

My stomach roiled. I turned so Cummings wouldn't see my face and lost the fight not to remember.

The way Willow had moved to Usher when I thought she had betrayed me made me sure that she knew how to use every situation to her advantage. I saw again how easily she had allowed his hand to find her breast and bile raged into my throat.

"Is there anything that ties her to Cadence Tait? Someone must have seen her downtown the night I did," I asked.

"Downtown's cleanin' up after the flood. The registration records from the motel where she was stayin' are probably ten miles downstream by now if that ain't in Kansas. Any tourist that might have seen her has headed for home." Cummings twirled the whiskey glass in his fingers.

I jerked at the words, and a pain stabbed my knee.

"After all the TV people got done telling us what a big hero she is, Cadence Tait left town." Cummings pinched the skin between his eyes with his free hand. "Probably on a plane to Iowa by now. Got her husband's body released, and the coffin is on the airplane with her. That woman knows people. Called in some favors, I'm guessin'." He let the glass dangle in his fingers. "It gets better. Highway patrol pulled Tommy Bumpus over just this side of Steamboat Springs." He looked at me and shook his head. "Now, get this. Tommy pulled a gun on the trooper. There's a shoot-out. Tommy took a bullet. He's in the hospital and not supposed to make it. If he don't pull through, there'll be nothin' to link all this elk poachin' to Batterton and Cadence Tait."

Like the strands of a rope, the pieces that I'd hoped to use against both of them snapped one fiber at a time. I thought of the one page in the notebook that could make a difference. Two names were scribbled on that piece of paper. "What about his brother?"

"Hayden made bail. He's long gone, too. But an elk poacher is not a top priority right now, what with the flood and all." Cummings tipped the bottom of his glass to the ceiling one last time. Breath hissed up from deep in his lungs and he wiped his mouth with the back of his hand.

"You should know this. The state crime lab in Fort Collins found the bullet in your truck. Matched it up to the bullets we found in the dead elk. Right now, it's the only thing we got, and it ain't much."

Cummings stood and walked to the kitchen. He paused and looked down at the map on the table. "You been studyin' on this?"

"Tryin' to put a picture in my mind of where the flood started."

He nodded. "I gotta get back." He picked up the whiskey bottle and screwed the lid tight.

"When all this is over, Hogan, let's you and me hike into Arrowhead Lake and catch us some of those big fish." He tugged on the end of his white mustache.

"That lake's covered with mosquitoes," I told him. "And this time of year, the bears will be feeding on the wild raspberries."

He held the bottle to the light and watched the whiskey swirl. "You're right. Bears don't bother me much, but I hate skeeters." He turned for the door.

"Wait." I started to stand, but the soreness clamped me to the chair. "When they got Tommy, did he have a rifle?"

Cumming's face twisted up in thought. "Report said he fired a handgun at the patrolman. What you gettin' at?"

"If it was a rifle, it could be the one he used to kill the elk."

"And?"

"It might match the bullet they found in my truck."

"If we could find it. Could be anywhere by now."

"Yeah." I leaned back in my chair. "I'm just trying for anything."

"If I find out more, I'll call you."

Cummings shut the door behind him. When his truck was gone, I eased up from the chair and went to the kitchen table. My finger found the little unnamed stream on the map. Did it lead to Tommy and Hayden's stash on the hillside? If it did, would Tommy have hidden that rifle there? And would it still be there?

And where was Batterton?

The map curled as I lifted Jenny's Bible from it. Jenny's doctors had teased us with words like remission. But cancer was a coward, hiding and waiting until its tentacles would reach out and twist a life away.

A teardrop puddled in the creases on the map. Jenny's Bible rested in my fingers for a few seconds more and I stroked the worn leather.

I had waited while cancer took my wife.

Cadence Tait was a coward. Batterton, a traitor. I wouldn't wait for them.

I took the onion skin paper receipt from the black book and held it in my fingers.

If that scrap of paper was found with Tommy's rifle—

Maybe I could put things in motion to ruin them. I could be the surgeon that could cut away the disease.

Jenny's Bible went heavy in my hands. I set it back on the table.

—

The prescription pain pills dulled the edge of the pain, but sleep wouldn't come. I tossed and turned with each new idea that seeped into my head. When the first new morning light played on the windows, I crept to the bathroom and let a hot shower wash over the purple bruises on my knee.

When I had dressed, I folded the map and tucked it into my shirt pocket. I found the pair of field glasses that Jenny had used to watch birds that came to our windows and stuffed them into a backpack with a canteen, a bag of trail mix, and the pain medication. In case I would need to explain why I was on the mountain, I took one of my fly rods and a vest from behind the door.

I tucked Willow's notebook in the pack. The scrap of paper that I could use against them was still inside. I was sure that if Cadence Tait felt the pressure, she'd turn on Bumpus, Usher, and Batterton. They had to be punished. They couldn't slip away. I wouldn't sit by and do nothing.

Jenny's Bible still lay on the table. I snatched it up, shoved it into a kitchen drawer, and asked her to forgive me.

Chapter Fifty-Three

On any other July morning, station wagons and campers would be lined up at the Beaver Meadows entrance to the Park. This morning there were only two other cars. Stories in the newspaper and on television speculated on the economic impact of the tourists fleeing the resort town. Hotel reservations were being canceled despite pleas from the Chamber of Commerce that Estes Park was wet but still alive and well.

A woman in a Smokey-the-Bear hat leaned out of the window of the entry booth window when my turn came. "You need to know Trail Ridge Road will be closed to all traffic today at noon. They're bringing equipment in from Granby to work on the bridge over Fall River," she told me. "Where you headed?"

"Grand Lake," I lied. "Will I be able to get back today?"

"You'll have to wait until tonight. The plan is to stop eastbound traffic at the Alpine Visitor Center until ten tonight." She tapped a finger on a large map taped to the wall behind her. "We need to keep people out while we handle the cleanup."

Fewer people would be better for my plans. "I won't be in the way."

And she waved me through.

I kept up with the cars in front of me for the first two miles, then I hung back and let some distance grow between us. At the junction on Deer Mountain, they hurried west, headed across Trail Ridge Road to Grand Lake, away from the confusion of a town digging out of the mud. I checked my rearview mirror to be sure no one was following and turned down the hill. I dodged around a barrier with a sign warning "Bridge Out" and headed toward Fall River, where I could start my search for the poachers' camp.

Around the next curve further down the hill, a park service truck blocked the road. A Ranger opened the truck's door, signaled for me to stop, and came to my side window.

"Sir, I can't let you go any farther." He leaned down and looked in. Even though his eyes wore the strain of too much work and too little sleep, he bobbed his head when he saw me. "You're Mister Hogan, aren't you? I was there when you came into the visitor center after . . ." He looked away. "What are you doing here?"

"I wanted to get a better look at what the flood . . ." I let my voice trail off. "I needed to see it again."

"Look, civilians aren't allowed down here." He rested his hands on my open window. "I'm supposed to write you a ticket for driving around the sign. I won't, on account of—" He shaded his eyes and squinted at the sky. "God, I hope we don't get any rain this afternoon. The ground down there is soaked. It could get really bad."

"I don't want to cause any trouble." I'd have to start my search from up above. "I'll turn around and get out of your hair."

"Thanks, Mister Hogan." He tapped a fist on the car door.

The smell of wet earth hung heavy in the air and a hint of sourness followed in the breeze. Jenny's stuffy hospice room had smelled so much the same.

In nearly thirty minutes, I made the curve on Trail Ridge Road to near where I had lost control of Willow's Corvette. Drag marks on the gravel shoulders showed where a tow truck had pulled the Corvette and the man's truck up from where Batterton and Usher had pushed them over the side. I moved my backpack closer to me on the car seat and touched the side pocket that held Willow's notebook.

I rolled down the window and listened for cars. When I was sure there were none, I swung off the pavement onto two faint, grass-covered ruts on a trail road used by the Hidden Valley Ski Area to maintain the ski lift. I followed the trail back into the aspens until I was sure a parked car couldn't be seen from the road.

I cut the engine and studied the map once more. The Bumpus brother's camp had to be in one of the unnamed, shallow valleys on the steep slope. It would have been easier to find by following the little stream up from the bottom. But these were the cards I'd been dealt. I locked the car behind me and swung the pack onto my back. I turned the collar of my jacket up against the morning chill and let the hate mask the stiffness in my knee.

—

Sweat streamed off my forehead.

You stupid old man, you'll never find it.

I hooked my fingers in the branches of a shoulder-high spruce and mopped my face with the other hand. I'd walked three—maybe four miles back and forth across the hillside, looking for some clue that my suspicions were right.

Nothing.

Like the fibers of a cancer hiding from a surgeon in healthy tissue, Cadence Tait and her murderers' evil hid in some wrinkle on this mountain I'd never find.

Too much ground to cover.

I slipped down to the ground and gulped water from my canteen.

Turn the notebook in. Tell them what you know. Let the authorities do their job.

Sweat stung the stitches in my knee and the joint throbbed.

You'll never find it. It might not even be here.

I dug into my pack for a handful of trail mix. My hand touched the plastic bottle of pain pills.

Take one. It'll take the edge off. Just one. Rest awhile.

I scooted into a shady spot under a tree, washed down two pills, and ate the rest of my trail mix.

Afternoon warmth swept over my aching muscles and the pills did their work.

Chapter Fifty-Four

My body jerked and my eyes opened. Brightness glared through the trees and shades of greens and browns blended. Sweat puddled along my collarbone and my shirt clung to my back and armpits. I heard a groan move across the still air. It came from me.

How long had I been asleep?

I lifted my left arm to look at my watch. Stiff muscles stretched.

The pills. That's why I slept so long.

It was ten after six. The few minutes in the warm sun had turned into hours. I shook my head to clear the clouds in my mind, but they draped over me like a summer afternoon storm on Longs Peak.

Nearly seven? *Crap.*

I had to get back to Jenny's car. Ardell would be checking on me if she hadn't already.

I was foolish. There was no way I could find Hayden and Tommy's hideout. Too many square miles to cover for a banged-up old man.

Even if it was somewhere on this mountain.

I pulled my knees up, reached back, and caught hold of the tree. Bracing for the pain in my knee, I eased myself up. The pills, the rest, and the warmth of the sun had done their job. The joint was stiff, but much of the pain was gone.

Ten 'til seven. It would be dark in two hours. I'd find Jenny's car, wait until I heard traffic on Trail Ridge, and then blend into the late-night travelers on their way back to Estes.

It was two miles or more to the road. Every bit of it uphill.

I lifted the canteen to my mouth. The water was warm from the afternoon in the sun. I knew I had eaten the last of the trail mix when I took the pills, but I checked anyway. A half of peanut and a broken yellow M&M hid in the corner of the Ziploc bag. I popped them in my mouth and hung the knapsack over my shoulder.

C'mom, old man, start walkin'.

—

Shadows from the pine trees crawled across the ground like long fingers searching for a prize. Faraway thunder rolled down the valley. I checked the sky. Angled shafts of orange light glowed on the skyline and afternoon clouds piled up on the peaks. The threat of rain hung in the air. I hoped all our prayers would be answered and that the heavens would hold back until the mud-soaked town had time to heal.

Chances were slim that the place where I'd left Jenny's car was directly above me. My best bet for finding the car would be to pick a route up the slope that would bring me to Trail Ridge somewhere on the uphill side of the hiding place. Then, when I reached the pavement, I could walk downhill until I found the maintenance road.

I took another sip from the canteen and picked a distant peak for my landmark.

Climb twenty steps, stop, two deep breaths, and then twenty more. Keep the pace slow and steady.

Count the steps now. One step . . . two . . .

—

. . . twenty . . .

Pale, green leaves whispered in a flutter of wind. The first whiff of rain drifted into the aspens around me. I checked the sky. Gray chased the high wisps of white to the east.

Then I heard a car.

The paved road was closer than I had thought.

I bit down on my lip, sucked in a breath, and readied for the next twenty steps. My fingers wrapped around the white bark of an aspen as big around as my wrist and I pulled myself up the slope. *One . . . two . . .*

From the sound, I knew the car was climbing the ridge. I strained to see a flash of sunlight off the car's windows, but the hillside was too steep for me to see anything above.

And the car inched along. Some patrolling ranger enjoying the sunset along the peaks, I guessed.

Nineteen . . . twenty.

My foot slipped back with a jolt and I bent to grab my knee. Two breaths, then go. Just two. I raised my face and drew a third breath. Now. *One step . . . two . . .*

Tires crunched on gravel. Was the ranger stopping?

Maybe the ranger had stopped to enjoy the last bit of the day,

Jenny loved sunsets on these mountains.

Seven steps—eight.

What would she think if she knew about this revenge I was plotting? Did my plan make me as evil as Cadence Tait and Batterton?

Hill's steeper. Stop at twelve this time. Just this time. Ten . . .

Maybe the ranger had spotted the mashed-down grass on the trail road where I'd hidden Jenny's car.

Twelve.

I hung my head and mopped the sweat away from my eyes. I sucked for air and told my heart to be quiet. The Ranger would hear.

Easy, old man. Breathe through your nose.

I caught hold of the rough bark of a pine to steady myself. A sour stench filled my nose. I lifted my face and sniffed again.

In the bent grass just a dozen feet from me, shiny black beetles swarmed into a rust-colored hole in the ribs of a dead elk. Insects had eaten the animal's eyes away and its hide strained across the bloated animal's ribs. The antlers were gone. Sawed off at the skull.

I gritted my teeth.

Even if Cadence Tait and Batterton hadn't pulled the trigger, the kill was theirs. The notebook in my pack told the story. Usher, Tommy, and Hayden, or men just like them in Wyoming and Montana, killed and hacked. There was a man called Ferris in Idaho who collected the antlers, then to Cho in Vancouver, then across the sea to Hong Kong and money came back to a bank in Ankeny, Iowa. The black book explained it all.

Was Willow a part of this too? I'd caught her in so many lies.

Usher had put a bullet in her and left her on this mountain like one of the elk.

No, it was me that left her. If I had tried harder, things might have been different. And Willow, if that was even her name, might still be alive.

Up on the road, a car door slammed. Feet crunched across the gravel shoulder and long shadows reached down to the aspens where I stood beside the dead elk.

"Batterton?" a voice shouted. "is that you?"

I dropped to my knees. My fingers touched a pile of hair that had sloughed off the carcass. The smell of decay turned vinegary on my tongue.

"What are you yellin' at?" a second voice called out.

"Thought I saw somethin' down there, that's all."

"We're early. Batterton never shows 'til it's exactly time. You know that."

"What you want me to do, then?"

"You walk down the road a piece,"—the voice laughed—"and leave me alone with the girl."

"You better hurry, Usher. We don't have much time."

I pressed closer to the ground.

Usher? The man I had fought in the bar.

The other voice had to be his friend from that night. The short one.

These men were here to meet Batterton? It made no sense. But there were three of them.

Run. Get out of here.

I glanced back down from where I'd come.

Stay in the shadows. Move slow. Hide. Then wait until dark. When they're gone, climb back to the road and find the car.

Girl? It boiled in my head. *Willow?*

It couldn't be. I saw the hole the bullet made in her stomach all over again. Cummings said they found her body.

No. Not her body. A woman's body. He said no ID.

Maybe she had escaped?

Shorty's footsteps walked down the gravel at the side of the road. After a few long seconds, Usher moved toward the car. The door opened.

"I'm back, Sugar." His voice was softer now. It flowed over the hill to where I hid. Then the car door shut.

I hated him. Like I hated him in those few minutes in the barroom as he pawed at Willow. I wanted the pool stick in my hands again. I remembered how it felt when it broke apart on his legs. I wanted to swing it again.

Is the girl Willow?

I was sure it wasn't. It couldn't be.

But these men were here to meet Batterton? That's what they'd said.

Usher's friend's footsteps moved farther away. I sucked in a deep breath, grabbed a handful of grass, pulled myself up, and started up the hill.

I scrambled up a knuckle-shaped rock outcropping at the edge of the pavement. Usher rested his head against the driver's window of a faded red pickup truck parked on the side of the road. I settled behind the slab of pink stone to watch and begged the pain in my knee to stop.

A blond girl stepped out of the truck.

I wanted her to be Willow. For an instant, I thought it was. But where Willow was tall and slender, this girl was short and thick. Willow was a woman. This girl was little more than a teenager. She moved away from the truck and turned to look back at Usher as she fastened her blue jeans under a roll of flesh on her chunky waist.

My stomach went sick. Had Usher used Willow the same way?

Or had she used him?

Then Batterton and Shorty stepped out from the forest at the front of the truck. "That was quite a show, Usher," Batterton said. "I told you not to bring her or any of your other girlfriends along when you workin' for me."

The old ranger wore dirty Levi's, and a torn shirt, and the same black cowboy hat was on his head as it had been the night he'd betrayed me. Perched on his shoulder was a set of antlers wrapped in burlap.

Usher's shoulders dropped. He eyed the girl and then

looked back at Batterton. "She begged to come along. I didn't think it would matter, seein' you said this is our last run."

The girl whirled around. Shorty covered his mouth with his hand and choked back a laugh. The girl stomped to the truck, climbed inside, and slammed the door.

I hunkered closer to the rock and held my breath.

Batterton swung the elk antlers off his shoulder. "Get with it. There's more just like these down that hill."

Usher snapped the buttons on his shirt closed. "This is the last time, right?"

"That's the orders. Get 'em loaded and get on the road."

"We gonna get our money first?"

"Ferris will pay you when you get to Boise. Missus Tait said to tell you there'd be a bonus this time."

Usher pulled on a pair of work gloves. "Seems like we're ending this too early. The flood scared most of the tourists out of the park. Rangers are too busy with the cleanup. It'd be easy pickin's. Still got a couple of weeks before the elk start rubbing the velvet off their horns." He flexed his shoulders and glanced at the girl in the pickup. "That's what they pay all that money for. Prime antler still in velvet."

Batterton stepped closer to Usher. "Do as you're told." Strings of spit hung from his mouth and flashed in the sunlight. "No one pays you to think."

Usher shrugged and stepped back. "Just talkin', that's all."

"You bring me my food?"

"Girl's got it. Brought you a six-pack, too. Thought you'd want that."

Batterton shook his head. "Two weeks ago, I was here when Tommy shot a big old bull just after dark. We found it piled up in the aspens down below here. I cut off the antlers and hung 'em in a tree. Big set. Bring a lot of money.

I'll go get those." He tapped on the windshield and waved at the girl inside. "Gimme a beer."

Batterton hooked his thumbs into his belt. "You two got a shitload of antler to haul up that hill."

"We're goin'." Usher nodded to Shorty.

Everything in the notebook was true. Tommy and Hayden killed the elk. Usher transported the antlers to Idaho. Batterton was up to his eyeballs in it. But Cadence Tait's name never appeared. It came down to that money order receipt. I had been right about the Bumpus's camp. Now Batterton was using camp as a hideout. That's why no one had seen him since the flood.

I blew out the breath I didn't know I'd held in. *Just wait. When they're gone, find the camp. Plant the receipt and call the Rangers. Let them hang for what they've done.* I shifted to ease the pain in my knee.

Over the edge of the rock, Batterton took a can of Coors from the girl and popped it open. Then he started down the road. He stopped not even thirty feet above me and looked over the edge to the aspen grove below.

Batterton tipped the beer to his lips. He gulped the can dry, tossed the empty over the edge, and then slip-slid down the gravel bank to the forest. Sun flashed off of the pistol tucked into a holster on his belt.

An icy raindrop splattered on my cheek.

Chapter Fifty-Five

Raindrops danced through the treetops. On the road above me, Batterton huddled under his cowboy hat and hunched his shoulders against the chill.

It was like something inside me said that as long as I watched him, he would not see me. It dared me. If I looked away, he'd see me.

In seconds, rivulets streamed from the pavement and down the hill to where I hid. Scraps of the velvet, from Batterton's elk's antlers, floated in the little torrents of gravel and mud. I thought of the Ranger's words from this morning and his concerns about what rain might do to the already-soaked ground in the valley and the muddy streets in Estes.

Then, just as quickly, the storm was over. New sunlight turned the wet droplets on the ground and in the trees into a million sparkling diamonds. A shiver coursed through my wet clothes and I wondered if God had answered so many prayers and stopped the rain.

Batterton craned his neck at the passing clouds and then clomped away into the forest.

Judging from the time it took Usher and Shorty to return from their first trip to get the antlers, their hiding place was closer to the road than I expected. The girl huddled in the pickup and never spoke to the men when they stopped to drop their burdens. She rolled down the truck's window and a plume of smoke curled from the cigarette that dangled in her fingers.

I scribbled the pickup's license plate number on my shirtsleeve. This was better than I had planned. I'd tell the police what I had seen here, give them the license number and when they stopped Usher, they'd find the truckload of poached antlers.

And if I could find the camp on this mountain and hide the black book and its little note. The evidence would lead the police to Cadence Tait.

Shorty and Usher made three more trips back and forth down the hill. The burlap bundles piled up next to the truck. Most of the antlers branched into five points. Those came from three- and four-year-old bulls. Others were spindly single daggers and ill-formed forks that came from younger animals.

Then Batterton called from the edge of the road. He stood in the shadows of the trees. A pair of antlers rested on his shoulders. I shrank back, wanting to hide but needing to see. The two men went to help him.

"Damn." Usher hurried to where Batterton waited. He took a long antler from Batterton. "You said he shot a big son-of-a-bitch, but I didn't expect anything like this." He set the base of the antler on the ground. The tip reached above his shoulder. "That old boy in Boise is gonna piss his Levi's when he gets a load of this pair." His hands traced the curves in the rough cloth wrapping like he was touching a woman. "This one alone will pay for the trip. Is the other one a match?"

Shorty heaved the second antler from Batterton's shoulder to the road. "It sure is," the little man said. "Seven points, just like the other, and I bet the set goes over two hundred and fifty pounds." He clamped both of his hands around the center of the antler and his stubby fingers failed to meet.

"Must be, what? Twenty thousand worth with all this?" Usher asked.

"Better be more than that." Batterton went to the truck and nudged the pile of antlers with the toe of his boot. "Let's get goin'. I want all the firewood out of the truck. We'll hide the antlers on the bottom and restack the wood on top and cover the whole thing with a tarp."

"Can't we just toss 'em up on top and throw the tarp over everything? We gotta get movin'. It'll be dark soon." Usher was at the truck's open window. He took the cigarette from the girl's mouth, moved it to his, and blew out a smoke ring.

"You heard me." Batterton dropped the tailgate and pushed an armload of wood onto the ground. "Unload this truck or you'll be workin' in the dark."

Now. Now, while they're busy. Find where Batteron's camp is. Hide the notebook. Wait until they leave and then call the police.

Shorty jumped into the back of the pickup and heaved chunks of wood over the side.

I eased back from the rocks until I was sure I was below the level of the roadway. Moving like a hunter stalking game, I skirted across the hillside until I found a place where I could see the skyline. An arc of pale sunlight hung against the black clouds stacked on the jagged mountains. It would be sundown in less than an hour.

At ten o'clock, the rangers would open Trail Ridge to a line of tourist cars waiting to return to the east side of the park. The timing was right. I could hide the notebook, climb back to the road, retrieve Jenny's car, and lose myself in the traffic making its way back to Estes Park. A call to the police with the license plate number of a truckload of poached antlers would start the clock moving.

Above me, the springs of their truck squealed and more wood fell to the ground.

Hurry. Before it gets dark.

I angled across the slope toward a thick stand of spruce trees where Batterton had gone to retrieve the big set of antlers. I slowed and picked each place to step. The snap of twigs or crunch of dried leaves under my boots could warn the men on the road that I was there. All went quiet except for the pulse in my temples.

From the stillness, a cow elk appeared in the brushstrokes of the coming twilight. Her still-spotted calf stepped forward, bending its fragile neck toward a place on the ground. I paused and watched as the young animal sniffed at the decaying, antlerless carcass of the bull these poachers had killed and left to rot. In the next second, the mother's eyes found me. She whirled and, without a sound, the two slipped away through the trees.

At least, Batterton and his hunters had spared these two.

Near the spruce, I found the scuffed places in the pine needles and dirt where Batterton had made his trips to get the hidden antlers. His tracks led down the hill, then turned sharply into the forest.

I pushed branches away, turned sideways, and stepped between the trees. A crushed beer can crackled under my foot. A squirrel chattered in answer. I jerked stock still, listening.

No other sounds.

Near the base of a thick spruce, Batterton's boot-prints stopped. A burlap thread caught on the spruce needles fluttered in the breeze, and on the ground. I could make out where strips of the spongy velvet had fallen from the antlers.

His camp must be close.

Spruce boughs brushed my face, and their pungent scent filled my nostrils. I studied the ground for some clue, but could find nothing on the trampled earth that would help. The evening breeze stirred the branches around me. The sound of moving water became clear. I pushed aside the spruce boughs and side-stepped between the trees.

Dirt crumbled beneath my feet. I snatched for a grip on the spruce branches to keep from falling. Hidden by the trees, there was a gash in the earth, no more than a foot wide. Water dribbled from a tangle of tree roots into a puddle the size of a skillet. Crystal-clear water collected in the tiny basin and then trickled down the hill. Miniature wildflowers and emerald-green moss decorated this primeval spot in the trees.

Betraying the fairyland, an empty Coors can stood upright in the water, like it had been tossed there by some evil giant. The monster's boot prints mashed the delicate moss. These were from Batterton's boots and the discarded beer cans were his. Hate rose in me. More than killing the elk, Batterton defiled the things he had vowed to protect.

A stride length away, another crumpled can marked the packed dirt of a trail following the stream downhill.

I looked up the hill toward the road and listened. Satisfied that the men were still loading the truck, I eased into the little gorge and followed the path beside the brook. In another few strides, this slice in the ground widened and cut into the earth. The path stayed close to the water and the walls of earth on both sides were as tall as my head. Cigarette butts lay among the tiny flower blossoms. More beer cans dotted the stream. Toilet paper stretched across a perfectly formed, foot-tall pine tree, and the stench of

Batterton's filth spoiled the air.

He's killing the earth like he killed the elk.

I hurried on.

Find where he sleeps. Hide the notebook. And get out of here.

Something moved across the ground above the pathway. I froze.

The elk with her calf?

No. They'd moved without a sound before.

Don't breathe.

The next noise floated through the air like a gasp.

No animal made that sound. What is it? Think.

It was the pop as if someone was opening a beer can.

Batterton had left Usher. He was coming back to his camp.

Dirt clods sprayed the edge of the ravine like hailstones.

Too late.

Batterton looked down at me. "Hey, whatya . . ." The beer can flew from his fingers and his foot lashed out at my face.

I caught the heel of his boot in both hands. With all the hate in me, I pushed straight up.

His arms shot from his sides to keep his balance.

I wrenched his foot downward

Batterton toppled into this slash in the earth. His stomach smashed into the dirt on the far side, trapping him half-in, half-out of the narrow crease. Air whooshed from his lungs and nose full of animal rage took control of the silence.

I refused to give up my grip on his leg.

He clawed for a hold in the dirt and struck out with his free leg.

I dodged his kick and wrenched down on his ankle until I felt the bone and sinew give way.

His hands lost their grip, and he tumbled hard onto his

back, smacking the ground with the sound of a ripe melon. He sprawled, face up, at the bottom of the cramped canyon beside the stream.

In an instant, I pulled the pistol from his belt and trained the muzzle at his face. But he didn't move. One knee was cocked oddly, and the foot I had ruined folded under him. Water from the little stream dammed at his shoulders, then rushed around his arm through the green moss and down the hill around my feet.

His head rolled to the side and droplets of blood trickled from his ear into the pool of water.

He's dead.

I lowered the pistol and reached down to touch his throat. A ragged breath hissed up from deep inside him. My hand snapped back.

He needs my help.

NO. NO. NO. He killed the driver.

He betrayed all he vowed to protect.

He ruined this place. He helped Cadence Tait, the Bumpuses and Usher kill the elk.

Willow's dead.

Hide the book and get out. Let the Rangers find him here.

I backed away two steps. Batterton's chest rose and fell in a ragged, regular rhythm.

Let him die here.

I backed away.

At the next turn in the pathway, a dirty sleeping bag spread out in a wide spot along the stream. A blue tarp had been tied between the trees to cover the campsite. Empty cans were piled near a battered Coleman stove and dirty clothes scattered over the ground. A vinyl rifle case hung from a tree branch.

I pulled the case down, tugged at the zipper, and slipped out the black steel and plastic of an Armalite carbine. At the end of the barrel was a cylinder-shaped silencer.

This was the gun they killed the elk with.

I took Willow's notebook from my back pocket, jammed it into the bottom of the rifle case, and pushed the gun back inside.

Now get out of here. Get home. Make the call.

I climbed out of the gully and zigzagged up the slope through the pine trees. With each step up, slanting shadows stole away the daylight and painted the forest gray. I passed the spot where Batterton lay, never letting myself look.

Muscles in my legs burned and my knee threatened to explode. I pushed harder. My heart pounded until I thought blood would spurt from my nose and mouth. I grabbed a tree to hold myself up and fought to catch my breath.

Out of the forest's quiet, I heard it.

"Help me." It was Batterton.

The man who I thought was a friend.

"Help me." So quiet and so loud that the words might make the mountain crumble and swallow the both of us.

Get away. Leave him.

I fought for my next steps up the hill.

Dead elk.

Paxton Tait drowned in the stream.

Blood dripping from the bullet hole in Willow's belly.

Every image twisted inside of me.

Like the fibers of cancer that stole my Jenny.

The cancer I could do nothing about.

I scrambled forward a few steps and stopped.

Don't give him a thought.

His bloody ear and broken leg filled the thoughts in my mind.

Leave him.

I lifted my face and listened for Batterton's voice. But

he was too far away now, or his voice was too weak, or he was—

Through the trees, a line of headlights followed Trail Ridge Road's curves down from the mountains.

I ordered my legs to move. Despite everything, they obeyed.

Up through the forest. Cars whisked by above me. I stumbled on the steep gravel below the road. When I tried to climb up, my legs gave way, and I fell. Sharp stones stabbed my knees and bit my palms. I crawled the last few feet up onto the road's shoulder.

Jenny, forgive me.

Lights flashed by. I raised onto one elbow and waved my arm.

Brakes squealed. A car pulled over. The door opened.

"Do you need help?"

I fought to stand.

"Mister?"

I'm sorry Jenny.

I slipped back onto the ground. The driver was closer now. He kneeled beside me.

I reached out and grabbed his hand. "A man's been hurt. We need to get help."

"Huh, what? You sure?"

New strength came from my words. "There's an emergency phone at the next turnout. Tell the Rangers what I said and tell them to hurry." I climbed up onto my knees. "Listen to me. Tell the Rangers, Hogan found Batterton." I looked into the man's eyes.

"Batterton," he repeated.

"Yeah, Batterton."

I struggled to gain my feet and turned back to the forest.

"Where are you going?" Confusion filled his voice.

"I have to help him."

Chapter Fifty-Six

The Ranger-boy's truck's headlights washed over the front of Jenny's house. "You sure you don't want to go to the hospital and get checked out?"

"I told you I'm fine."

"Maybe you oughta—"

"I said I'll be okay." I jerked up on the door handle as the truck rolled to a stop.

"Let me help you get inside."

"No."

"Okay." He handed my backpack to me. "Mister Hogan"—when I pulled on the pack, he held it tight—"I heard one of the paramedics say that Batterton could have died if they wouldn't have got to him when they did. I heard 'em say you pulled him out of the water, wrapped him up in the sleeping bag, got a fire going. Probably stopped hypothermia. Not many folks would have gone back down that hill."—he relaxed his grip on my knapsack—"Awful brave of you. You should be proud of yourself."

Brave? Proud? I swallowed hard. "You would have done the same thing."

"I'm not so sure. If you woulda left Batterton on that mountain all alone, I don't think many people from around here would have said a word. Soon as he gets outta the hospital, he's going right to jail." He nodded at the house. "You sure I can't help you?"

"I'll be fine." I hung my head. "I just need some sleep, that's all."

"Okay, then. American Horse said she'd call you in the morning and work out a time for you to make a report. Good night, sir."

I wasn't brave. There was nothing I should be proud of. I had almost become as evil as the men I hated. Tears mixed with the dirt on my face and fell in great brown drops on the stair steps to the front door.

The clock on the mantle struck two. I found Jenny's Bible from the kitchen drawer where I'd hidden it and put it back in its place on the kitchen table. I washed down two of the pain pills, switched off the light, and fell back into the Lazyboy in front of the fireplace.

—

At the first ring of the phone, ragged pains fired every joint. I reached for the receiver.

"This is Hogan."

"Dad?"

The pain in my hands and knees left. At the same moment, my anger and confusion faded. "Jennifer."

"Dad, I've been trying to call since we heard about the flood. Everything's okay, isn't it?"

"Yeah, Jenn. I'm fine. I'm sorry I didn't call."

"Jess and I've been so worried. I bet she called me a hundred times."

"I'm fine." Awkward, but we were talking. "I promise

I'll call her as soon as we hang up."

"Good. I know she wants to hear from you. I told her that you were probably out helping someone who was hurt by the flood. That's what our dad does."

Tears came. "Jenn, it's so good to hear you."

"Dad, there's something else. Allen and I were going to wait to tell you but—We found out for sure Tuesday—Oh, Dad, we're going to have a baby."

The words stuck in my throat, but they were the only words that could be said. "Your mother would be so happy."

Chapter Fifty-Seven

I went to Fall River the day before I was to testify.

Autumn's first yellow showed in the pockets of aspens on the slopes high above the river. Giant boulders that had tumbled from the mountain in the flood dotted the valley floor. Delicate new grass sprouted from the black silt that had been swept into the valley.

I was drawn to the place where I had met Willow. The place where we found the man's body. And I brought my flyrod.

Today, anger didn't come with me.

Like before, I knelt behind a fringe of weeds. Careful to keep my shadow off the water, I swung the four-weight rod back over my shoulder, chose just the right ripple to place the caddis fly, and arched the rod forward.

A car door slammed.

Dalton Cummings climbed out of his pickup and quick-stepped down the rocky bank from the roadway. He picked his way through the clumps of stunted willows to where I knelt by the stream. "When you weren't at your cabin, I thought I might find you here." He pulled his Stetson from his head and smoothed his white hair. "They won't need you tomorrow."

"It's over?" I looked back at the river and watched my fly catch the current.

"To save his own neck, Usher spilled his guts. When Tommy found out, he copped a plea. Blamed everything on his brother. Said Hayden killed Paxton Tait 'cause he thought he spotted him shootin' elk. Said that the next morning his brother shot at you to give you a scare. He admitted to the poachin' but blamed everything he could on Hayden." Cummings knelt and moved the palm of his hand over the tips of the new grass. "What with his brother in the ground, only Tommy knows for sure who did what. They're guessin' the judge will give him three to five. He'll be out in two. If that long."

I raised the tip of the rod, picked the fly off of the water, and tossed it back upstream. "Hayden didn't say anything about Cadence Tait and Batterton, did he?"

"Didn't. Or wouldn't. We'll never know." Cummings reached out and plucked a smooth stone from the riverbank. He played it through his fingers until I looked at him. "Batterton got himself a high-dollar lawyer. His lawyer got him a deal. That kind of lawyer doesn't care about what's right."

I turned back to the river.

"Don't even think about it, Hogan." He plopped the stone into the river. "God don't need help being God."

Dalton tilted his Stetson.

"One more thing. Right after the judge sentenced Hayden, this news-reporter fella rushed in. Seems this morning Cadence Tait was killed by a hit-and-run driver in downtown Des Moines."

The river's chill wicked through me.

"Listen to this." He wiped his forehead with the back of his hand. "First reports say she was run over by a woman drivin' a red Corvette."

"Willow?"

"You're forgettin' we never found no record of anyone named Willow Stanford and we still don't know whose body it was they pulled out of the river after the flood." Cummings stood up. "Hayden and Usher both said that the woman—Willow or whatever her name was—had all the records of the poaching in a black notebook. Like the one they found in the gun case at Batterton's campsite. You wouldn't know anything about that, would you?"

I cocked the fly rod back, swung forward, and laid the line on the water. "No."

"Didn't think so." He gave the brim of his hat a tug. "You think of anything else, Hogan?"

I reeled in the line and held out my hand. Cummings took it and helped me to my feet.

"There is one more thing." I looked him in the eye. "I'm going to be a grandpa."

He cocked his head and studied my face, then winked at me. "You'll make a good one." And he left me by the river.

The black silt the flood had left would nourish the new grass. Elk would come to the meadows beside Fall River to feed. September would bring tourists to watch the great bulls gather their harems. Then winter would cleanse this valley with snow. In its time, elk that never heard the poacher's rifles would graze in these meadows and another generation of vacationers would gasp at the beauty of the mountains. Even the raw gouges in the soil and rocks on the mountainside from the Lawn Lake Flood would heal.

And so would I.

I shook out my fly line, picked a spot, and made the cast. The caddis settled on the water, caught the current,

and glided down the stream.
    I whispered Jenny's name.
    And the river answered back.

Here's a peek at the first chapter of Guy Hogan's next adventure, *Early Snow*.

Chapter One

Sunday, October 30, 1982

By noon, the autumn sky had turned from blue to the color of road asphalt. Treetops bent in the winds that funneled from the high peaks down into the canyon. Stray snowflakes splattered the windshield, turned into tiny droplets, and in an instant were gone.

My best friend and new boss, Dalton Cummings, pulled his pickup into a spot at the back of the big white hotel's parking lot and killed the engine. "The truck with the paintings is supposed to be here in about an hour." He pulled up the sleeve of his flannel shirt and checked his Timex watch for the tenth time. "Let's leave our gear here. I'll let the hotel manager know we're ready. You see if you can find,"—He snatched a clipboard from the dashboard and flipped through the pages—"damn it, I can never remember her . . ."

"Porsche Hurt," I told him. "Porsche. Like the car. Hurt, like ouch."

"That's one of those damn made-up New York City names if I've ever heard one. Her folks never gave it to her."

"You've said that before." Then it hit me. I held back the smile. "I know what's going on. Ex-game warden Dalton Cummings is nervous about his first paying job since retirement. What could it be?" I enjoyed the edge I had over my friend.

Cummings turned toward the window. His breath painted a gray haze over the glass.

"Let me guess." I wanted to see his face, but he wouldn't look back. "The man who fought forest fires, rescued lost campers, and saved fish and wildlife for generations to come is afraid of a New York woman."

"That ain't it."

"Then what?"

He shook his head and the brim of his Stetson left a mark on the fogged window. "I don't like hotels," he mumbled.

"What?"

"Hotels." He clamped both hands on the steering wheel. "I'd rather be in my own bed." He stared straight ahead. "I do fine in a sleepin' bag in the backcountry. But there's somethin' about a little old mint on a fluffy pillow and turned-down sheets that makes me all crawly." He shook like he was cold. "It's all too fancy."

"Don't worry." I bit back a laugh. "It's just two nights. You probably won't get any sleep, anyway." I couldn't resist adding one more thing. "The ghosts will keep you awake."

Cummings jerked up on the door handle and glanced sideways at me. He raised his middle finger. "Screw you, Hogan."

—

A handful of dried leaves skittered from The Stanley Hotel's front doors across the lobby's hardwood. Smoke from the fire that crackled in the fireplace blended with the scent of bacon and warm maple syrup on the plates of the guests enjoying a late breakfast in the MacGregor Room. A white-haired couple sat on a Queen Anne loveseat and watched the first snowflakes through the lobby's picture windows. Her head rested on his shoulder.

Except for the white Reeboks on the old man's feet, it could have been a scene from the first dozen years after The Stanley opened. My wife had told me that she would have enjoyed that more genteel time. When women chose their best dresses and dined on china, with crystal and silver. When blue jeans were reserved for the afternoon trail rides and tennis shoes were worn only for tennis. During our vacation nights in the old hotel, we made plans to move to Estes Park. I had even told Jenny that one day I could see myself working at the old hotel—perhaps leading the historic tours or suggesting places to fish for the guests. But things had changed. Jenny was gone. But a small part of those dreams had come true. I'd be working at the Stanley Hotel for the next two nights.

A man in a dark blue blazer with brass buttons tossed another pine log into the fireplace and turned his back to enjoy the warmth.

I tugged at the zipper of my down jacket and crossed the lobby to where he stood. "I'm with Cummings Security. Here to help with the art show. I'm Guy Hogan."

"Jim Colton, Mister Hogan." He pushed a shock of faded blond hair off his forehead. "They told me to expect you." His eyes narrowed. "Am I right? You were the one who helped solve that elk poaching scandal up in the park. About the time of the Lawn Lake flood? A woman was killed. Do I remember correctly?"

I bit down on my lip and nodded, then held out my hand.

Colton's grip was soft, and his face was tired from too many years of being too polite to too many people. "My boss is letting your manager know we're here," I told him. "I'm supposed to find Porsche Hurt and see what she needs for us to do 'til the truck arrives."

A round woman in a shiny purple jogging suit pushed in between us. "Excuse me." She looked up at Colton. "I'm supposed to be on the hotel tour. You know, the one that shows us all the haunted places and tells us about the ghosts," she panted. "I lost track of the time—too many prunes at breakfast—have they left yet? The tour, I mean."

Colton's attention went from me to the woman. "Mrs. Randolph, isn't it?"

"*Mizzz* Randolph." She took off her eyeglasses and left them hanging from a beaded chain around her neck. She batted her eyes at the concierge and patted the gooey nest of gray spikes that was in her hair.

"Yes, *Ms.* Randolph. The tour just left. You can catch them downstairs."

"Have I missed anything?"

"No. But you'll need to hurry."

She fumbled with her glasses. "Was that Odyssey Pruitt I saw outside? You know, the artist. She was all bundled up, but I'm sure it was her."

Colton focused on the woman as if she were the only other person in the room. "It very well could have been. I saw her in the lobby earlier this morning. She was an employee here at the hotel several years ago, so she's familiar with the area."

"I know all that." Ms. Randolph lowered her voice. "I'm one of her biggest fans. I already own two of her paintings. I intend to buy another one at her show." With that, she waddled across the lobby and down the stairs.

The concierge smiled at me and shook his head.

"Odyssey?" I asked. "That's whose paintings I'm going to be guarding?"

"Yeah. It was Audrey when she worked here. Strange girl. A mousy little thing who kept to herself. She"—Colton's fingers made quote marks in the air—"found herself. Started painting. And changed her name somewhere along the line. They pay me to know such things." He peeked over his shoulder at the registration counter. "Though this weekend I was asked not to tell that bit of story with our guests."

The front doors opened. Two women in ski jackets and scarves stood in the opening. A bellman with an overloaded luggage cart stopped short of running the two over.

Colton nodded at the door. "Looks like I'm needed."

"Porsche Hurt?"

"Follow *Mizzz* Randolph. Ms. Hurt's with the ghost tour."

"How will I know which one is her?"

"Oh, you'll know her. She'll be the only woman less than sixty in that group." His eyebrows arched. "And Mister Hogan, she's something to see."

—

Three more women as round and colorful as Ms. Randolph squeezed into the narrow corridor at the bottom of the stairway. The floor cocked slightly off level and someone had removed the light bulbs from every other fixture down the hall. Even at nearly noon, the corridor seemed as shadowy as twilight.

The ladies jostled closer to a tall man in the same blue blazer as Colton's. His hair was as gray as everyone around him. Somewhere in the middle of the group, an arm raised and the blaze from a flashbulb filled the hall.

The tour leader blinked but never lost the rhythm of his well-practiced spiel. "This location was selected for this hotel not only for the view of the valley, but because the natural limestone and quartz formations could be used as the foundation for this glorious building. It is well known that quartz is a conductor of physic energy. That would be one of the factors that make his hotel very special."

Ms. Randolph nodded, and a smile beamed from her face.

The leader gestured to a padlocked door marked *employees only*.

Ms. Randolph pushed by the other ladies for a better look. Her bright nylon jogging suit swished as one of her thick thighs rubbed the other.

The tour leader went on, "In the early days, this hotel was quite isolated and the staff was housed in buildings behind the main structure."

Ms. Randolph stood on her tip-toes and waved her hand to interrupt the man. "Is that where Odyssey Pruitt lived when she worked here?"

"Why, yes."

"Will we—"

"We will discuss that when we view the employee dormitories." He cleared his throat and gave a quick sideways glance to the other ladies. "As I was saying, tunnels were built to connect the hotel with the staff housing. During construction, there was a cave-in, and one of the workers was killed." It went very quiet. Even Ms. Randolph's nylon ceased. "Today, our marketing and purchasing departments have their offices on this level. Just a few weeks ago, one of the staff, who had stayed to work late, swears they heard the sound of a hammer striking stone." He paused. A practiced pause, I guessed. "Could it be that the trapped soul of that worker is still seeking to escape from his cold tomb?"

Ms. Randolph's hand covered her mouth, but a tiny gasp escaped.

"If you'll count with me, that is the first of the seven ghosts we'll discuss on our tour."

I wasn't counting. I needed to find Porsche Hurt. If what Colton had said about young and attractive was true, she wasn't part of this group. I glanced at my watch. The truck with the paintings was due any minute. Cummings would be looking for me. Given his mood from earlier, I needed to find Miss Hurt soon or get upstairs now and tell him I hadn't.

Another round of flashbulbs popped. The tour followed their leader toward a shaft of daylight shining through the window of a ground-level door at the far end of the hallway.

From an alcove, a woman I hadn't seen before stepped out. She could have been one of the hotel visitors from those gentler times. A pale gray skirt fell to just below her knees. Ruffles on the front of her blouse rippled when she moved. Perhaps this was ghost number two. But her high heels tapped over the rough concrete floor. She paused; her face hidden in the glare of one of the lights. Her hair was blonde, and the lights made it golden.

There is a socially accepted length of time a man can look at a beautiful woman before that stare becomes a gawk. I was dangerously close to breaking that rule.

I swallowed and mustered the strength to call out. "Miss Hurt?"

The woman turned; her face still lost in the harsh shine.

Before she could speak, the door at the end of the hallway burst wide open. Like the whistle of a runaway locomotive hurtling through a tunnel, a lady's shriek filled the hallway.

"Odyssey?" Ms. Randolph reached out to the figure who had screamed. "Dear, what's wrong?"

I was moving toward the open door before I realized it.

In the narrow hallway, I shoved past the woman in gray, around the ladies in the tour, and by their leader. Ms. Randolph's arms wrapped around the small woman who'd come from the outside. "Odyssey. Child, what is it?" she asked.

Snowflakes matted in Odyssey's hair. She buried her face in her hands. The tips of her fingers were bright with blood.

"Odyssey?" Ms. Randolph squeezed her tighter.

The girl pulled her hands away from her face. "Someone," she gasped out. "Someone cut off his head."

—

Someone cut off his head.

Snow swirled off the building. It hung in fresh, new clumps on the pine tree branches and covered the lawn near the hotel. I could make out Odyssey's footprints, but fluffy flakes as big as quarters quickly covered the marks.

Someone cut off his—

She'd seen a body. The blood on her fingers was bright red.

I grabbed the frame around the open door and looked at the young woman in Ms. Randolph's arms. "Odyssey, where is it?"

She raised her face from the woman's shoulder. Melted snow and tears blended with streaks of dark make-up on her cheeks. Her eyes stared at me but seemed to see nothing.

I made my voice softer. "Where is it, Odyssey?"

Her lips trembled. "The tree. The big tree."

Between the building and a gazebo where tourists gathered on summer nights stood a pine tree taller than the fourth-story windows of the hotel. I squinted into the flurry of falling flakes, pushed off the door frame, and started for the tree.

Someone—

That someone could still be out there.

It was two dozen slick steps to the pine tree. Its branches had been trimmed away as high as a man could reach, and a wooden bench rested against the trunk. Stalks of autumn-dried wildflowers dusted with white crowded near its base.

A severed head. There would be blood. Lots of blood.

But no red stained the white. No headless body covered in the falling snow.

I sucked in what might have been my first breath since Odyssey screamed. With the toe of my boot, I swept away the snow near the old bench. Nothing.

Voices and the rustling sound of nylon on nylon moved behind me. I whipped around. The ladies from the tour huddled together, watching for what I would do next. Odyssey was still in Ms. Randolph's arms.

"Where did you see it, Odyssey?" I spoke softly.

She raised her arm and pointed.

Just where the path turned toward the hotel, fading footprints left their marks where someone had stopped. Just a bump in the snow.

Not a body. Bile rushed into the back of my throat. *Only the head.* Snowflakes collected on the upright hairs on the back of my neck.

"Go on back to the hotel. All of you," I said over my shoulder.

No one moved.

"Please, go back inside."

They stayed rooted to the place they stood.

I dropped onto my knees with my back to the ladies, shielding them from the horror I was about to uncover.

It's small. Too small to be a person's head. What if? No. It can't be. A child's head?

My mind formed a prayer. I reached out and brushed

away the thin layer of new snow. The hair was wet. And brown. I pushed more snow away. Relief let my shoulders drop.

"Ladies, it's a dead rabbit." Brown-gray fur and a white cotton-ball tail. I turned to the group. "Odyssey, did you see this rabbit?"

She pulled away from Ms. Randolph and nodded. "But someone cut off its head. The spirits did it. I know they did. It's a warning. They don't want me here."

The woman in gray stepped between the ladies and where I knelt. "Enough excitement for now." She spread out her arms and waved her hands toward the hotel. "Go on inside before we all freeze." She wrapped her arm around Odyssey's shoulder and gave a squeeze. "It's just a rabbit, dear. Some old coyote was hunting for his dinner, that's all. Happens out here all the time. You remember."

Ms. Randolph tugged on Odyssey's coat sleeve, pulled her close, and wrapped her arm around the girl's waist. The two followed the others into the hotel.

I looked down at the dead rabbit. The woman in gray was right. The flower gardens and bushes around the hotel were a perfect place for rabbits to hide. Coyotes or foxes might slip in at night and pick off a cottontail for their supper. Something could have scared this one off before it could eat its kill. What she said made perfect sense.

Except that the coyote that killed this rabbit carried a knife.

The rabbit's head had been sliced neatly off, and I couldn't find it anywhere in the snow nearby.

The woman in gray moved closer to me. "None of those ladies will sleep tonight." Droplets from the melting snow clung to the ends of her hair and collected in the folds of the lace on the front of her blouse. In the shadowy hallway, the light had made her hair shine like gold. Outside it was the color of caramel. Faded freckles played across her high cheekbones, and her eyes were brown. I had been right to stare at her in the hall.

"Yeah, I'm not so sure I will either. Sleep tonight, I mean." I was staring again. Maybe gawking. And this woman knew about coyotes. "You're not Porsche Hurt, are you?"

"No. My name is Shelby Guess. I work for the hotel's marketing department. I was just coming out of my office when—" She nodded toward the rabbit in the snow. "And you are?"

"Guy Hogan. I'm with Cummings Security. Here to help with the art show."

"That's why you asked for Porsche. I see now. I work in marketing for the hotel and I'm the liaison for the event." She shivered at the cold. "Let's go inside and I'll help you find Porsche."

"Let me take care of this." I pointed at the rabbit. "Give me a minute and I'll meet you."

She turned and her long legs carried her quickly over the snowy ground, back to the hotel.

I scooped up the rabbit. Rigor mortis stiffened the little body. It had been dead for some time. Dark blood seeped from where the head had been cut from the neck, not like the fresh blood that stained Odyssey's fingers. No tear marks on the fur. No holes from a predator's teeth.

Maybe it was the spirits.

I fished a paper bag from the trash bin outside the hotel door and slipped the dead rabbit inside. I tucked the bundle under the trash can.

Maybe I'd show this to Cummings. Just to see what he thinks about a headless rabbit.

It wasn't the cold that prickled my neck when I reached for the door handle to go inside. It was that feeling that someone was watching.

Jim Colton stood at the corner window of the floor just

above me. He stepped back when I raised my face.

Author's Notes

Rocky Mountain National Park is a real place. In 2022, over four million recreational visitors came for beauty, wildlife, and adventures. The Lawn Lake Flood of July 1982 left marks that are still visible today and sparked the thoughts that became this novel. Estes Park and Grand Lake are the east and west gateway towns to Rocky Park. Trailridge Road connects the two towns and is the highest (in elevation) paved road in America. This author attempted to knit those very real places into a story that people would enjoy and perhaps, remind them of trips to Rocky or entice them to consider a visit.

Next, what do people imagine when they think of an author?

Do they see a solitary figure hunched over the glow from a laptop? Does the writer lift their head and grin after composing a clever description? In frustration, do they hit the delete key and begin their writing again? Do they swallow the lump in the back of their throat upon rereading a particularly emotional scene they have just typed?

This author thought of late nights, all alone, creating the next blockbuster. He would slide the finished pages under the door and mail from astonished readers and checks from New York would slide back in. This writer discovered that he needed others around him.

Thank you to professional organizations such as Western Writers of America, Mystery Writers of America, and particularly, Rocky Mountain Fiction Writers. More appreciated than the organizations are the valued friendships that grew from the people I met. Thanks to the revolving cast of characters that filled the chairs around the table at Thursday night critique sessions. Much appreciation for the WOTB group that zooms in on Monday nights. Suzie Q you're the best. Of course, thanks always to an enduring and forgiving wife.

Finally, the backdrop for TRAILRIDGE is where I live and, I must confess, the novel is a little about me.

www.kevinwolfstoryteller.com

About the Author

Kevin Wolf's novel, THE HOMEPLACE is the winner of the 2015 Tony Hillerman Award. The novel was a finalist for the 2016 Strand Critics Award for Debut Mystery. Western Writers of America selected his short story, BELTHANGER as the 2021 Spur Award Winner for Best Short fiction. The great-grand-son of Colorado homesteaders, he enjoys fly fishing, old Winchesters, and 1950s Western movies. He lives in Estes Park, CO with his wife. Visit his website: www.kevinwolfstoryteller.com

www.ingramcontent.com/pod-product-compliance
Lightning Source LLC
Chambersburg PA
CBHW022124310726
48972CB00007B/2178